Fidā-é-Lucknow

Fida-é-Lucknow

Tales of the city and its people

Parveen Talha

With a foreword by Muzaffar Ali

NIYOGI
BOOKS

Published by

NIYOGI BOOKS

D-78, Okhla Industrial Area, Phase-I
New Delhi-110 020, INDIA
Tel: 91-11-26816301, 49327000
Fax: 91-11-26810483, 26813830
email: niyogibooks@gmail.com
website: www.niyogibooksindia.com

Text © Parveen Talha

Editor: Gita Rajan
Design: Misha Oberoi
Layout: Sarojini Gosain / Niyogi Books

ISBN: 978-93-81523-70-4
Publication: 2013

Printed at: Niyogi Offset Pvt. Ltd., New Delhi, India.

In memory of my parents,
Enayat Maryam and Mohammad Talha,
through whose eyes
I saw Lucknow

View of *Kallan ki Lat*, a British cemetery in Lucknow,
captured from the balcony of the author's home in 1984.

Contents

Foreword

When Parveen writes she literally holds you by both hands and walks you through pages of time that were intimately left open for her. She takes you on a journey into a way of life of a bygone Awadh and through the milieu, she knows so well, weaves her way into the emotions and gets you hooked on to the plot. She is so enamoured by what she wants to share with the reader that she takes nothing for granted, leaves nothing to chance. Even when she is not holding a pen, her eyes are beaming with a story to hear and a story to tell. I have had the rare experience to work on a short digital film 'The Shawl', based on a story by her, and recreate an ambience of a Lucknow which we grew up in. The story has been included in the book. I have also associated with her on a twenty-seven-part serial Husn-é-Jaana set in nineteenth-century Qasbati Awadh. Fascinated by her childlike, romantic and rational imagination I often brainstorm with her on story ideas for films.

This collection of short stories will unfold the beauty of an Awadh that the next generation yearns to be a part of. She rediscovers those footprints that have been erased from the sands of time.

Muzaffar Ali
December 2012

Preface

Much has been written about Lucknow and that incredible 'tehzeeb' which left the world gasping. But the Lucknow-wala who took the Indo-Persian culture to the pinnacle of refinement got lost under reams of fable and legend. He does surface sometimes in a Bombay movie as a paan-eating, Sherwani-clad, half-lunatic Nawab, squandering millions on a quail fight or on a *tawaif*. I must admit Lucknow has had its share of the ridiculous. But for God's sake! Could a *tehzeeb*, which the world refuses to forget about, have evolved unless the city's share of the sublime was predominant? It is time the real Lucknow-wala got the spotlight on himself.

For me the real Lucknow-wala is not just the man of the soil but one who came to Lucknow from any part of the world and got involved in building that glamorous Ganga-Jamuni culture which lives today in legend and history and also in the memories of some people. He may be a Muslim, a *Kayasth*, a *Khatri*, a Kashmiri pundit; educated or uneducated, a nobleman, a tongawala or a sweeper, an Indian or a European.

So let's find out his qualities, his characteristics, and his nature. How is he different from people of other cities? What is it that makes him stand out? Is it the hyperbole in his language?

The exaggeration in his hospitality? The drama in his humility? Yes all this, but these are just the outward manifestations of a culture. There is something within the nature of these people which make them different. They are a sensitive lot. In their lives a word given to another or tradition established by an ancestor are like principles, to be abided by religiously even at the cost of personal discomfort or loss. When he establishes a relationship he wants to carry it till the end of his life. When he makes sacrifices for another he does it casually without making much of it. He does not parade his own woes. He hides his sufferings behind a mask of happiness and refuses to talk about them, just as he understates his own qualities.

It is surprising how the Lucknow-wala has become known as a person who is relaxed, fun-loving, and unconcerned about serious things. He has really never had it all that easy, as is believed. His leading role in the mutiny of 1857 made him stand for punishment till 1947, and thereafter, the results of the Partition took over. Lucknow (Muslim) families were torn apart just as those of some other North Indian cities. Those who went to the new country never really found a home there, and those who stayed behind had to pay for belonging to a community which had insisted on the Partition. In the post-Partition period the neglect of Urdu and its avoidable death left the Lucknow-wala broken. Finally, what he prized most, the Hindu-Muslim unity, was poisoned by the pulling down of the Babri Masjid in 1992.

Even nature does not spare him. Year in and year out there have been floods which ravage the homes and fields of people. Three floods of the 20th century have been of unusual magnitude. People still talk about the floods of 1960 when boats plied in Hazratganj and also about the 1971 one, when even Butler Palace, where senior state government officials lived, was under water. The first flood of the 20th century, which caused unbearable damage and left innumerable people homeless, was in 1915. Many had to leave Lucknow to find shelter elsewhere. Naubat Rai Nazar, a poet, was one flood-hit citizen who refused to leave Lucknow. Even in a moment of extreme helplessness he wrote a *sher* which became very popular and acquired the status of a classic:

> *Kya hai taqat asman ki jo chhudae Lucknow*
> *Lucknow hum pe fida hum fida-é-Lucknow*

[Even Heaven does not have the strength to take (me) away from Lucknow. For Lucknow loves me with a passion and I love Lucknow with a passion]

The owner of *Awadh Akhbar*, a very popular newspaper of Awadh, was so impressed with this *sher* that he gave an award of Rs 50/ and a gold ring to the poet and invited him to work for his newspaper.

The skyline of Lucknow has been changing at such a rapid pace in recent years that the citizen cannot be blamed if he finds his memory unable to retain old images. It is not just the structure of the city which has acquired a new look but the social set up and values have also changed to a great extent. The city stands transformed drastically. For this no one should be blamed. The world is marching ahead and so is Lucknow. As one new image superimposes itself upon another, and is replaced by yet another, like a video cassette fast-forwarded, one wants to stop somewhere and rewind to the times when clocks did move but also left traces behind. It is not exactly nostalgia which persuades one to rewind but there is an intense desire to decipher those traces, and footprints on the face of time which gave the city dignity, variety and colour. In 2011 some people got together and decided to restore to Hazratganj its original look. A Herculean task, no doubt, but they were successful.

It was Chandra Prakash of Universal Book Sellers (a shop in Hazratganj for more than seventy years) who convinced the traders of the Ganj to take up the cudgels to restore its past glory to the bazaar which had not only given them bread and butter but a place of respect in the city. He then got like-minded people of Lucknow under an umbrella called 'Connect Lucknow' and together they persuaded the U.P. Government to take up the project. By 2012 their efforts bore fruit. From a defaced market, emerged the Ganj of a long forgotten era, in all its elegance, in all its grace.

In every nook and corner of Lucknow, in every movement of the hands of the clock I see a story, which I want to share with others, but I was never sure whether anyone would understand the ramblings of a person's mind who herself is a child of the change which invaded the city. At last I gathered courage to present before readers a collection of stories, written over a period of 35 years, about Lucknow and its citizens who love Lucknow like no other city is loved. The book carrying stories of such people can only be called "Fida-é-Lucknow".

Parveen Talha
December 2012

A Mother Divided[*]

Dinner over, Mubarakun lay down on her large cot with her five-year-old twin sons on either side waiting for her to tell them a story. "The king called his wazir and said...." Mubarakun began the story. Before she could finish her sentence, her son Akkoo grabbed her chin and turned her face towards him. "What Amma, you never look at me when you are telling a story," he complained.

Mubarakun was about to turn towards him when his brother Saggoo shouted. "No Amma should look at me." Saggoo always spoke with authority, but when it came to his mother's attention Akkoo would not give up either. "Amma will look at me," he insisted, without raising his voice.

"She will not." Saggoo screamed. "She will look at me."

"No, at me," Akkoo retorted.

"At meee."

"At me, meeee."

Just when it appeared that the brothers were about to start a fight, Akkoo, with the softest of smiles spread over his face, asked,

---

[*] This story has appeared in the *Telegraph* Colour Magazine on 9 March 1986 as Fiction selected by Khushwant Singh.

"Amma, why can't you look at both of us, when you are telling a story?" Saggoo agreed, "Yes Amma look at both of us as if we are one." Mubarakun felt the world at her feet. "*Mere Bachchon*," she said and took both her sons in her arms and nestled them close to her breasts. In a little while both were fast asleep and could not care less what the king had said to his wazir.

The kids fought for their mother's attention all the time. Yet, strangely enough, while each child wanted the mother for himself, neither wanted to deprive the other of her attention. Even while they were breastfed, they had insisted on being fed together, each had marked one breast for himself and would not touch the other. This partitioning of their mother's breasts amused the grownups of the family, but not Mubarakun. She chided them for quarrelling over her but noticed that they could not do without each other. Mubarakun often wondered whether her sons, as grown up and married men, would still love her and each other with the same intensity. Unfortunately, she was not destined to see what the future held for her sons.

The boys were barely seven, when an attack of malaria took Mubarakun away to the land of the dead. The little boys filled the atmosphere with their heart-piercing cries. "Amma, come back, we promise we will never fight over you again." But Mubarakun never came back nor did the sparkle in her sons' eyes. That was dimmed forever. But gradually, perhaps to make up for what they had lost, the brothers drew closer, than ever before, to each other. They went to college, married, had families of their own, but continued living under the same roof, eating from the same kitchen. They were inseparable. This went on for thirty-three years.

Till the year 1947.

It was in the spring of 1947 that the first portent of the disaster that was to follow was seen in the joint households. One evening, Akkoo burst into the house in a state of despair. Heading straight towards Saggoo's room, he said, "You know Saggoo, I have just heard some leaders addressing a large gathering in Aminuddaullah Park. They were saying that Muslims should be driven out into Pakistan." Saggoo turned pale but he tried to calm his brother. "Look Akkoo, there are a handful of communalists who are trying to create trouble. This should not upset us." But Akkoo looked shaken.

The next morning the two brothers stood face to face with Mukundlal Rastogi, a rich moneylender of Lucknow. He had come to buy their house. "But we are not selling our house," both the brothers said in an equally stunned voice.

"You will, when you leave for Pakistan." Rastogi explained.

"We are not going to Pakistan," only Akkoo could find words.

"You will, ultimately, Doctor Sahib, all wise Muslims are leaving," Rastogi said and went away. His words echoed in the minds of the two brothers long after he left.

The same evening, Dr Balraj Sinha, a colleague and dear friend of Akkoo, telephoned to thank him for doing the night shift. "Life would be difficult without you, Akbar. I hope you will never go to Pakistan, although I know you will have better prospects in your own country," Sinha said.

"India is my country," Akbar's voice sounded hurt.

"Sorry, I meant a Muslim will be better looked after in a Muslim country."

Akbar wanted to say that he had been looked after well enough so far, that the country where he was born and where his ancestors were born was his country, and that he had every right to live and die there. But he said nothing. In the days that followed, such incidents confronted the brothers at every step.

At last the twins, who had so far thought alike, found themselves reacting in different ways to these incidents. Akbar became convinced that they should cross over to Pakistan and find a new home. Doubts crept into his mind about the Hindus around him and about the new government. He wanted to give the Muslim League a try.

Asghar, on the other hand, refused to bow down to such fears. He wanted to continue to live where he was living. His motherland was where he and his ancestors were born and it could not be shifted according to the whims of politicians. This was how Asghar and perhaps a few other individuals thought. But crowds, even in the otherwise peaceful Lucknow streets, shouted, "*But ke rahega Hindustan,*" and "*Hans ke liya hai Pakistan, ladke lenge Hindustan.*"

Gradually, in the midst of bloodshed and frenzy the year 1947 moved towards its end, leaving behind bitterness and broken families. For Akbar and Asghar, too, the year could bring only a feeling of pain, very similar to the one which invaded their tiny beings at the time of Mubarakun's death. The breaking point came when their aunt, Rehmatunnissa, left.

"I wonder what Lucknow will be worth without *Khala Amma,*" Akbar remarked. Saggoo said nothing. He was fighting hard to control his tears. Rehmatunnissa was the only source of affection, after Mubarakun's death, for the brothers.

They had hardly recovered from the shock of their aunt's departure, when their very dear doctor friend, Shafi, was killed by Hindu fanatics in the Kumbha Mela where he was sent to fight disease. Akbar became desperate to leave India. He refused to see reason. It was then that Asghar played the trump card which he had so far kept in reserve. "If we go away, who will light a lamp or say *fateha* on Amma's grave?" This argument had the desired effect on Akbar. One could see blood draining away from his face. Before Asghar could complete his argument, Akbar broke down. Both the brothers wept like children. For the time being, such discussions were suspended.

For a few more weeks life continued as before in their household. But the country groaned with pain. Lucknow was apparently peaceful, but people even there were full of fear. In such an atmosphere, Akbar was one day called by a young Hindu to see his ailing wife. Akbar was examining her when the patient's mother stormed into the room and tried to prevent him from touching her, "All *Musalmans* are butchers," she shouted and cursed her son-in-law for calling a Muslim doctor into the house. Akbar had to leave. The patient's brother escorted him to his carriage. "Doctor Sahib," he said on the way, "times have changed. My mother's fears are not all that baseless. Perhaps, you too should not have come into a Hindu house unescorted." The young man's words first spread a wave of shock on Akbar's face and then hardened the expression into that of determination. "Medical college?" the *coachwan* asked Akbar as he climbed into the carriage. "No, Mubarak Manzil." Akbar was going back home, perhaps to leave it forever. That evening when Asghar came back from the court, he found his sister-in-law busy packing. Akbar was helping her.

"We are leaving for Lahore on Friday," announced Akbar. Asghar looked at his brother's face and knew that there was no scope left for argument or reasoning. He knew his brother well, but he also knew his own mind. "And I am not leaving," he said. The sound of a death knell could not have been more terrifying than Asghar's words for Akbar's ears and for his own.

The inevitable happened. Friday came. Namaz over, the two brothers went with their families to Charbagh railway station. Two hours later, Asghar and his family walked back alone to an empty house. Akbar and Asghar lived for many years thereafter, but their paths never crossed each other again except for one brief interval.

In the balcony of a multi-storeyed building two old men sat on garden chairs. Before them lay the vast city of Karachi and behind them seventy packed years. The two bore the same name but belonged to different countries.

"Is not Karachi very different from Lucknow, Saggoo?" one old man asked the other.

"Lucknow too is very different from the one you knew, Akkoo," the other replied.

"Is Aishbagh any different?" the first one asked. The Muslim graveyard in Lucknow was in a locality called Aishbagh. But the question referred, not to the graveyard, but to a specific grave where a young mother called Mubarakun lay interred for sixty-three years. These men were her children. They were the inseparable twins – Akbar Abid Hussain, the doctor and Asghar

Abid Hussain, the lawyer. They had met after thirty years. Akbar was eager to know the condition of his mother's grave.

Immediately after Akbar's departure to Pakistan, Asghar had found a gaping crack across the centre of his mother's marble grave. "And what about the land on either side of Amma's grave which we had bought with our first earnings for our final resting place?" Akbar asked.

"It is there, waiting for us," Asghar said.

"That wish of mine, like so many others, does not show any sign of being fulfilled." Akbar looked a picture of pain. Asghar decided to talk to him in a lighter vein.

"Don't worry, your government will allow your body to be carried to Lucknow. You see, governments care a lot for people's sentiments," Asghar joked.

"If that is so, how is it that you took thirty long years to come and see your twin brother?" Asghar for once, found himself speechless. It was a fact that for many years after the Partition, Asghar's loyalty to his government was doubted. His applications for a passport to Pakistan were turned down. To crown it all, he had run out of money. His legal practice had dwindled and his house was attached as evacuee property and sold to a Sikh refugee from Pakistan. During those years, Asghar's concentration was on the education of Tayyaba and Tahira, his two daughters, who in years to come qualified for the top civil service of the country and became known among the senior officers of the state. It was only then that Asghar could pull the right strings for getting the passport.

On the other side of the border, Akbar never got back the flourishing medical practice of the Lucknow days. Eking out a living for seven children totally drained his health. He was advised not to travel. In short, destiny, by its devious means, saw to it that the brothers did not meet till then.

"At least we have met, things could have been worse." Asghar continued to be an incorrigible optimist. "If I had come a couple of months later, you would not have been in Karachi but in Canada."

"Well yes, that is what the children want." Akbar replied. All his children had migrated to Canada. He was curious why Asghar's daughters had never thought of settling in the West.

"Because they did well in India. Things have improved enormously for the Muslims over the years," Asghar informed him.

"But they haven't found husbands," Akbar reminded him.

"Yes, that is true, one does not find many young Muslim men doing well so far. But things will be better in future," Asghar said.

"How will that help Tayyaba and Tahira and others of their generation?" Akbar asked.

"Well, they will have to remain unmarried or be prepared to marry men of other communities, or perhaps be satisfied with unsuitable spouses."

"Are Muslim men that rare in India?" said a shocked Akbar.

"The Partition has thrown communities apart. And for that, we are responsible," Asghar explained.

Guilt spread over Akbar's face and a long silence followed. After some time Asghar picked up the threads again, "Yes, we, because we allowed ourselves to be carried away by a handful of politicians who did not know what they were up to."

"We didn't have a choice. Our misfortune was that we got leaders who chose to experiment with the destinies of a generation," Akbar explained.

"And that generation was doomed. Whether it was you, Akkoo, who crossed over to Pakistan, or whether it was me, who stayed behind. We both suffered," Asghar said and paused, then added, "and the sufferings of one generation cannot be erased by the gains of the next."

"I hope no other community makes this mistake, ever again," Akbar prayed.

"Carving out a nation on the basis of religion does not solve any problems, at least not the minority problem," Asghar said.

Over the years the two brothers had learned to live in the past. They, like many of their generation, spent a lot of time thinking and talking about the events which led to the Partition and hoping that those events may never be repeated. This mental preoccupation with those events had its reasons. There were millions of families who, even after thirty years of Independence, did not find a home like Akbar's family, which was still on the move. His children had moved from Pakistan to Canada from where they sent him a visa but Akbar dreaded going there. "If you don't want to go to Canada, then don't," Asghar said.

"There is not much left here either. A country where the government can declare the devoutest of Muslims as kafirs cannot be a very comfortable place to live in." Akbar sounded so morose that Asghar decided to write to Tahira. She had once told her father that on compassionate grounds the nationality of an individual can be changed. When Akbar heard about this he looked happier than he had done in the last thirty years.

"But don't have very high expectations from the government there either," Asghar said and both of them had a hearty laugh.

Since that day the brothers were often heard talking about the future, the future that would be at home in Lucknow where both of them would be together at last, and so near their mother's grave. Both started dreaming once again of getting their final resting place near her. But providence again decided otherwise. Akbar developed fever and pain in the chest, after coming back from a walk one evening. Old age loses resistance to fight even minor ailments. With each day Akbar's condition deteriorated. He died on the sixth day and was buried in Karachi, a thousand miles and million barriers away from where Mubarakun slept.

Immediately after the burial, Asghar left for Lucknow, where he still lives in Mubarak Manzil, which was originally his and Akbar's, but was declared evacuee property sometime after Akbar left for Pakistan. Now he pays rent to a Sikh refugee, from Pakistan, who had claimed it from the custodian in place of the property he had left behind in Sialkot. He spends most of his time in the Aishbagh Muslim cemetery, with some mason or the other, trying unsuccessfully to fill in the crack which appeared on his mother's grave years ago.

Badi Dulhan

There was a time in Lucknow when eating paan was taboo for unmarried girls. But the Qazi would hardly be out of the room after hearing the "*Hun*" as consent from the bride when she'd pounce on the nearest *paandaan* and never leave it again. Husbands found it convenient to share their wife's attention with the *paandaan*. They gave them "*paandaan kharch*," which literally meant a stipend to maintain and run the *paandaan*, but which was really pocket money for the wife.

The ladies made fresh paans and chewed them when at home and served them to their visitors. When on social visits some carried their own brand of prepared paans in a pretty metal case wrapped in a damp cloth, normally bright red in colour. The other ingredients like chewing tobacco, betel nuts, cloves and cardamoms would be in an ornate cloth pouch called *batwa*.

But Badi Dulhan did none of this. Even when on social visits she carried the whole *paandaan* with her. She liked her paans fresh and she liked to prepare them herself. She was convinced no one else could put the right ratio of ingredients in the paans the way she could. She would often say that only when Allah

Mian sends her an invitation would she venture out of her home without a *paandaan*!

I knew Badi Dulhan since my childhood and always looked forward to her visits. Her coming to our house meant a breakfast of *tinki* and *namish* for the whole family. There wasn't a single occasion that I know of, when Badi Dulhan came to our house without these delicacies. The practice, my father told me, was started by Badi Dulhan's mother-in-law who came once, long long ago, in the morning when father was barely seven. His mother had just passed away, and the old lady found him crying for *tinki*, the rotis prepared with flour kneaded with ghee and milk and *namish*, a sweet dish prepared of whipped milk after exposing it overnight to frost. She felt that the motherless child did not get enough indulgence, recalling that his mother always gave him a breakfast of *tinki* and *namish*. She left the house immediately on her waiting *doli* and returned in no time, with an earthen pot overflowing with *namish*, and paper thin *tinkis* wrapped in a white napkin. Never again did she cross the threshold of our house without those delicacies. After her death her eldest son's wife, whom she called Badi Dulhan, made that practice a tradition.

Over the years, Badi Dulhan's money matters took a downward trend as was obvious by the replacement of her silver *paandaan* with a big copper one. Soon the big copper *paandaan* became smaller and smaller. At her last visit to our house, it had acquired almost the size of a toy *paandaan*. But she was too proud to share with anyone the tensions of this new phase in her life. She was a complete stranger to poverty and yet, she had that rare ability to draw a curtain over it.

Over the years something else also happened. While *namish* survived in Lucknow, after being rechristened *malai makhan*, *tinki* became extinct. There were few khansamas left who could make those paper thin *roghni rotis*. But we continued to have our breakfast of *tinki* and *namish* each time Badi Dulhan visited us.

Today Badi Dulhan is here again, an old lady well past her eighties. She walks into the Balrampur Hospital where my father is being treated for a sluggish liver. The doctors have been insisting that he should be made to eat somehow, just anything. For they see danger in his blood pressure sliding down uncontrollably. But food is anathema for him. He cannot look at it, he cannot hear about it. His liver is obviously refusing to respond to treatment. His only nutrition is glucose and Dopamine which is given to him intravenously round the clock.

Father's face lights up into a smile as he makes an effort to get up when he is told that Badi Dulhan has come to enquire about his health. His voice acquires its previous strength and volume, God only knows from where.

"*Adab baja laata hun*, Badi Dulhan. I am sure you haven't forgotten my *tinki* and *namish*."

She hadn't! The graceful old lady moved towards the bed with a tray on which is placed an earthen pot overflowing with foamy frothy *namish* and paper thin *tinkis*, wrapped in a white napkin. Father made an effort to get up. The doctor, who is incidentally in the ward, helps him and encourages him to have as much as he wants. A look of satisfaction spreads on the doctor's face. His patient has eaten, of his own free will, after a very long time. His appetite has obviously revived.

Everyone is happy and so is Badi Dulhan. She settles down, relaxed and peaceful, on a chair facing father's bed, and takes out a ready-made paan from a paper packet and gently slips it into her mouth. I am taken aback to see a paper packet of prepared paans in Badi Dulhan's hands! Even the little copper *paandaan* which she carried till sometime ago is not there anymore. In a flash something hits me.

I have guessed how Badi Dulhan arranged for those *tinkis* and *namish* this time. I rush with a heavy heart, and place myself between Badi Dulhan's chair and father's bed. I don't want him to see Badi Dulhan's empty hands. Not in his condition. But he is already asking her, "Badi Dulhan, why aren't you eating a fresh paan? Where is your *paandaan*?"

"Don't expect these frail hands to carry a *paandaan*," Badi Dulhan replies with mock irritation and adds, "and you better get back home fast, I don't like hospitals. I am not going to come here again." Then, showering everyone in the ward with blessings and good wishes, and sounding as cheerful as ever she makes her exit, but leaves behind a trail of heavy hearts.

The Shawl[*]

When I saw a crowd outside the haveli, I knew I was too late. Two of Dulhan Begum's sons came forward and helped me from the rickshaw and escorted me to the *zanankhana*. I reached when Dulhan Begum's body was being lifted from the bed and put on a wooden plank. *Nawan* was ready with lukewarm water to give Dulhan Begum her last bath.

As the lady relatives stretched bed sheets round the place, *nawan* slowly removed the clothes from the body, an extremely difficult task to perform on a dead body. Dulhan Begum's faded blue shawl which was warmly wrapped round her head and upper body proved particularly difficult to remove even for *nawan's* expert hands. Dulhan Begum was perhaps holding on to the edges of the material when she breathed her last and that clasp had now frozen into eternity. Scissors helped to relieve her of that fabric but two tiny bits of blue continued to peep through her clenched fists even as her body was lowered into her final resting place.

Before they took the body away, the face of the dead woman was exposed for a brief moment for all the dear and near ones to

* This story first appeared in the *Hindustan Times* weekend supplement in 1978.

have a last look. It was then that I saw on her face an expression which I had longed to see in all the fifty years that I knew her. I saw life.

This strange woman was known to me for half a century. I met her first, a couple of years after she entered Sirajuddin's haveli as his bride. Her mother-in-law addressed her as "Dulhan Begum" and that she remained till the end. Her husband and servants and later on, her children and grandchildren, and anyone who addressed her, called her that.

I was employed by her rich barrister husband to teach her English. Those were the days when ambitious Indians thought they could further their contacts by introducing the language of the rulers within their *zanankhanas*.

I found Dulhan Begum extraordinarily receptive. In fact within a couple of months, I feared that I might have to look for another job. I celebrated the successful completion of this assignment by inviting Dulhan Begum for a cup of tea to my house. She arrived in a one-horse carriage in all her regal splendour. On this occasion, just as a gesture of friendship, I asked her her name. She settled her silver laden *dupatta* on her raven tresses, raised her beautiful eyelids and looked at me. I saw her eyes. They were painfully expressionless. And I heard her say, "I was Sakina, now I am Dulhan Begum." She paused, and looked up again, with the same pair of dead eyes, "Continue to call me Dulhan Begum." Her voice, like her eyes, was expressionless, but I got the message. Perhaps like all aristocrats of Awadh she too allowed familiarity to the chosen. But my contacts with the family did not end there. After Dulhan Begum, her children and nieces continued to be God's excuse for my bread and butter. And then a time came when the wall between the employer and the employed dissolved and I found myself a part of family.

Children and grown-ups alike flocked round me on my visits. Dulhan Begum was the only one who maintained her distance, but that she did even with her seven children and her doting husband. Between Dulhan Begum and me conversation never progressed beyond a passing exchange of salutations, as I would raise my right hand and mumble an "*Adab*" her lovely eyelids would gradually go up, revealing those large expressionless eyes for a split of a second and then she would resume her work. But the momentary unveiling of those eyes never left me happy. I would spend hours thinking of those dead eyes and the expression which never changed with the occasion. I hoped in vain to see a change of expression in those eyes on the seven occasions when she brought a child into this world; on the occasion when Sirajuddin escaped an accident which could have been fatal. On the occasion when she lost one of her five sons and finally when Sirajuddin left for the next world. On none of these occasions, when any other human being would have been distorted with ecstasy or grief, did I see any change in those eyes or on that face.

Only two incidents come to my mind when Dulhan Begum had reacted like a living human being. The first one was when I decided to marry Albert and leave Lucknow for Calcutta. As courtesy demanded I went to Dulhan Begum to inform her of my decision. She mumbled the customary good wishes and resumed her work. Just before I left the room her daughter came in carrying a slip of paper on which I had written Albert's address which was to be my new home. God only knew how Dulhan Begum's eyes travelled to that slip of paper. And then I witnessed for the first time a strange light spread into her eyes, her lips stretched into a smile and then I heard a voice which vibrated like a very sad tune. "You will live on Shamsul Huda Road in Calcutta?" Surprisingly there was envy in her voice.

"Do you know the place?" I asked.

"Yes," she said and with that, the earlier expression came back to her eyes with a jerk.

The other incident took place years later when I was visiting the family on the occasion of the circumcision ceremony of one of Dulhan Begum's grandsons. Her daughter-in-law, who was being pestered by the *coachwan's* wife for some warm clothes, handed to that woman, Dulhan Begum's blue shawl. The shawl definitely had worn off by then and could have been easily dispensed with. But Dulhan Begum did not think so. "How dare you touch any of my belongings without my permission?" Dulhan Begum who was known for her generosity and detachment to worldly belongings, thundered and then dissolved into tears.

Sirajuddin had never witnessed a sight like that. He pulled out a *pashmina* shawl from his own wardrobe, ran to the *coachwan's* quarters, gave it to the *coachwan's* wife and came back to Dulhan Begum with her faded blue shawl. For a moment the eyes shone with a strange light and the lips stretched, and then all was as before. And then today, as they lifted the white veil from Dulhan Begum's shrouded body, I saw an expression of life more real and definitely more lasting than on the earlier two occasions. I cannot define that look on her face. It was both of relief and of joy. And as her four sons lifted her pier and walked with heavy steps towards the burial ground, I felt I saw Dulhan Begum alive for the first time in the last fifty years that I knew her.

After the funeral rites were over, in spite of the sincere persuasion from the children I could stay no more in that haveli. I left Lucknow on the third day.

Months later, back in Calcutta, Albert and I went with our son Tony to see his wife Patricia off, at the Howrah railway station. Patricia was on her way to see her parents. After the train started moving Tony realised that Patricia's thermos flask carrying milk was left behind in his hand. He ran with the train and managed to hand over the flask to his wife. I admit that it was rather reckless of Tony to have done that, but the way Albert lost his temper was also not called for. "Tony's concern about his wife's comfort is not all that unnatural, Bertie," I addressed my husband as we came out of Howrah station after Tony moved ahead to hail a taxi.

"Agnes you seem to have put your seventy years in a safe deposit somewhere. You live in a teenager's world! Which wise man would risk his life for the comfort of a silly woman who pretends that she cannot look after herself?" Albert refused to see reason.

"What do you mean some silly woman? Pat is Tony's wife..." As I was about to lose my cool, Albert controlled himself. "Sorry my dear, I am really sorry. When one is no longer young one only sees the darker side of life. I was afraid history might repeat itself. Agnes dear, we cannot afford to lose Tony for anything in the world." I saw fear staring at me through Albert's eyes, and when I saw apology spread over his wrinkled face, I found the effect heart-breaking. All I could do was to put my gnarled and withered arm around his bent back to suggest that he was forgiven. Tony led both of us into the taxi which he had just brought. Throughout the drive Albert was quiet, but I could see reminiscences flitting past his eyes. I wished I could know which incident in his life was the one which he did not want to be repeated. On reaching home, just before we retired for the night, Albert's mood had changed. He appeared eager to talk.

"Do you know Agnes, the evening before Mohsin caught the fatal influenza, both of us had gone to see-off his wife at the Howrah railway station." In the last thirty-five years of our marriage Albert had spoken about his childhood friend and neighbour Mohsin so often that I knew about him almost as much as Albert did. I knew that Mohsin had married his childhood playmate, and that their love for each other was almost legendary. I also knew that when the influenza epidemic claimed his life just six months after his marriage, his young wife was left a broken person but surprisingly she got married to a rich man from Lucknow even before the next Id-moon was sighted. All that I already knew but today Albert was eager to tell me more. He continued to talk about that December evening the memory of which had not faded for him even after fifty-one long winters.

"The train moved," Albert spoke with enthusiasm, "and Mohsin realised that his wife's shawl was left behind in his hand. He chased the train, just as our Romeo did today. As I stood holding my breath between my teeth I saw two awestruck eyes almost falling off from the curtained compartment imploring Mohsin not to bother. But Mohsin did not give up. The train was far beyond the yard when a bejewelled hand managed to hold on to the blue shawl. That was the last communication between Mohsin and his beloved wife." Albert said with an air of finality about him but he had not completed the story. That very evening Mohsin developed a fever and high temperature and all the symptoms of the killer influenza came over him. On the fourth day he was no more.

"But running on the platform had nothing to do with his getting the disease. You have told me before that the epidemic had spread," I tried to calm Albert so that he may not draw any more comparisons with that incident and Tony's running with the train.

"I know that, old girl! I am only trying to convey that on Mohsin's priority list his wife's comfort was placed higher than his own life," Albert said and then added with a sigh on his lips and contempt in his eyes, "and that very woman grabbed the hand of another the moment the opportunity appeared."

"Albert, you talk as though you are not aware how helpless Indian girls can be before the wishes of their parents and society." God alone knows why my heart melted for the girl-widow of more than half a century ago, and I asked, "What was her name?"

"Sakina." Albert's voice fell on my ears like a bombshell and suddenly many a faded scene from my Lucknow days laden with the dust of time, emerged before my eyes. And as Albert talked I could only see two dead eyes staring at me from a blank expressionless face.

Albert continued to talk. He told me the moment Mohsin realised that the fatal disease had struck him he talked and thought only of Sakina. Even the thought of his old and doting parents did not make him as restless as the idea of Sakina's life without him.

"Everyone will sooner or later rehabilitate themselves but not Sakina. The flowers will never again bloom for her." This was one of Mohsin's last utterances.

"This was how he viewed Sakina's future without himself. And how entirely wrong he was! Sakina went through spring and flowers all the way," Albert said and gave a cynical laugh.

"Oh Albert how can you jump to such cruel conclusions! Mohsin was absolutely right. Spring did come but the flowers never again bloomed for Sakina," I was almost hysterical.

"How are you so sure?" Albert was rightly perplexed.

"Because I know it," I said, between my tears.

The Plans of Allah

Sharafat Ullah was a tongawala. He lived in Hussainabad, not far from the Clock Tower. His ancestors also lived in that part of Lucknow, and like him plied tongas for a living. Sharafat was proud of his ancestry and his profession. He was proud, above all, of his horse Sheikhu. He believed that Sheikhu was the fastest, smartest and greatest of all horses in Lucknow, one who didn't deserve to be tied to a tonga. Sharafat was not wrong there, only guilty of a little exaggeration. In Lucknow speech without hyperbole is no speech.

Sheikhu was tall and well built. In his younger days he could run twelve miles in an hour, carrying the weight of a tonga all the while, with four well fed men sitting on it. For most part of his life, Sheikhu helped Sharafat earn quite a fat amount to keep his family in comfort. For years Sharafat's *dastarkhwan* had a meat dish both at lunch and dinner. The food was always enough for the large family. They ate as much as they wanted. Once in a week Sharafat would run to the market, early in the morning, and come back loaded with jalebis and bananas. His children loved jalebis for breakfast and Sheikhu loved bananas. Sheikhu was a well fed horse. He ate three kilos of gram soaked in water, and loads of fresh grass, which was delivered to their house by a grass cutter. In winters he was given butter too with chapattis. A refreshing oil massage by Sharafat was a daily feature all the year round. Sheikhu appeared as happy with life as was Sharafat and his family. In the evening when Sharafat and Sheikhu came back home after a day's hard work and Sharafat had disengaged him from the tonga, Sheikhu would stand up on his hind legs and touch his forelegs on Sharafat's shoulders and neigh several times. That touch and that neighing would take away Sharafat's fatigue and fill him with ecstasy. The neighbours who otherwise envied Sharafat's life loved to watch that scene – the most eloquent expression of love for a human being by a creation of the Almighty who knew no language.

Sharafat's children also stood around to watch the scene every evening and were indeed touched by the horse's expression of love. Yet neither of his two sons wanted to follow their father's profession. Sharafat didn't mind. He realised that his profession had no future in Lucknow. The city was stretching beyond recognition. It was no longer just Hazratganj, Aminabad and Chowk, as it was in his childhood. Mahnagar, where people went just once in a year, to see the Tazia burial in the Sunni Karbala, and Aliganj, where pilgrims gathered on Bara Mangal, were already big colonies where the rich lived. Fast moving vehicles were the need of the times.

"In another ten years, the tonga will be pushed out," Sharafat thought, but he was wrong. The tonga had long lost its popularity with the rich. Even the educated youth felt embarrassed to be seen on that vehicle. Sharafat had noticed the change, but not the speed at which the change had come.

And the speed was likely to become faster with time. Lucknow roads were no longer moving with rickshaws, tongas, and *ikkas* but were racing with hundreds of varieties of cars, tempos, three-wheelers, buses and trucks. Only experts like Sharafat could manipulate a tonga between those fast vehicles on roads, far narrower now, thanks to the widespread encroachments.

Sharafat's income had remained steady so far, mainly because of Sheikhu's stunning physique, the well maintained tonga he was tied to, Sharafat's choice of the routes from where he picked his passengers, and his interesting conversation with them. Sharafat was totally uneducated, but he could speak chaste Urdu, having lived with educated families where his father and grandfather served as *coachwans*. He had learnt the correct history of the Nawabs and knew stories from *Tilism Hoshruba*, which his grandfather would regale him with at bed time, when he was a child.

Sharafat found good husbands for his three daughters and married them off in style. He placed his two sons as apprentices; one in a shoe factory and the other to learn *zardozi* embroidery. For Sheikhu's future too, Sharafat had spun such plans which, perhaps, were never ever woven for a beast of burden. He was determined to relieve Sheikhu of all work by the time he was thirteen. He longed to see Sheikhu resting, with no burdens to carry, just galloping around in the jungle behind his house.

But very soon two realities dawned on Sharafat. One, that the jungle, where he had dreamed of Sheikhu galloping around, had remained a jungle, no doubt, not of green trees and creepers, but of concrete. Sharafat was shocked and was totally shaken, at the second revelation. He woke up to the fact that Sheikhu was already twelve and just months away from his thirteenth birthday. Sharafat came home with a sinking feeling, dejected and disappointed. His self-confidence had never touched such a low ebb before. He cursed himself, "I am no good; Sheikhu will soon be thirteen and I have not saved enough, to buy a younger horse. I have frittered away all the money which Sheikhu earned for me, and I have done nothing for him." His sons, Yusuf and Yunus, noticed the dejected look on their father's face and made enquiries, "What is troubling you *Abba*?" Yusuf asked, and Sharafat poured out his grief.

"*Abba*, don't worry," Yusuf said, and Yunus agreed, "In a month's time, we will start getting our daily wages. Buying a younger horse will be no problem then. You will be able to buy one in a year." Sharafat recovered his optimism and strength with that one sentence from his sons.

The coming year meant harder work for Sharafat and Sheikhu. Sharafat's wife ran the household very frugally, they managed to save enough. But the savings were spent not to buy a younger horse, but on the weddings of their two sons. The parents noticed that Yusuf and Yunus were keen to get married. They saw wisdom in not insisting on the plans Sharafat had for Sheikhu's old age. With a heavy heart he put Sheikhu's retirement on wait.

Retirement could wait, but not old age. Sharafat noticed that Sheikhu's reactions were not so quick any more. It was his fifteenth year. Most of his life was spent doing real hard work. Sharafat shivered when he recalled that Sheikhu's mother Gulbadan had passed away when she was fifteen and her father and grandfather, who led a more comfortable life, had also lived to just about that age. "Ae Allah! Give my Sheikhu a longer life, and a little rest, in this world, too. He has worked tirelessly for me and has expected nothing in return." That prayer was on Sharafat's tongue with every breath.

But all prayers are not answered by Allah according to plans which human beings make. Allah has his own way of answering them. This prayer of Sharafat was answered thus: Sharafat had dropped a few passengers at Gol-Darwaza in Chowk and was heading towards home. He was so close from his house that the Hussainabad Clock Tower had emerged before his eyes in full view. Just then, a car came from behind at a speed of more than 100 km per hour. It brushed against the left wheel of the tonga toppling it along with the horse on the side of the footpath. In the process Sheikhu's forelegs were seriously injured. That was the end of Sharafat's dreams. His plans came crashing down. Sheikhu could stand up after four long months and could never again pull a tonga. He just limped around. Most of the time he stood in his shed looking a picture of life gone by.

Sheikhu was given the best medical treatment available, thanks to a very competent compounder at the Government Veterinary Hospital, who lived not far from Sharafat's house, and whose child Sharafat had dropped and picked up from school for years. His meals had also so far been looked after, with what remained from Sharafat's savings after his sons' weddings. But the future was uncertain.

Soon a warning came from Sharafat's sons. "*Abba*, till you start working again, you and Amma can have your meals from my kitchen and Yunus'. There will be no shortage for either of you. But you know what our wages are; can we buy three kilos of gram and loads of grass for Sheikhu?" Yusuf said and Yunus stood nearby, along with his wife and Yusuf's, nodding his head.

"I know *Beta* that is why I have already arranged to hire a cycle rickshaw. I will start pulling it from tomorrow. You two will not have to bother about your parents nor Sheikhu," Sharafat said with great optimism and started his new work the following day. But he realised, on the very first day, the vast difference between plying a tonga and pulling a rickshaw. As a tonga driver, all that he did was to sit on the front seat with the reins in his hand, and occasionally a whip, and steer his way through the traffic. Pulling a rickshaw was to do what poor Sheikhu had been doing. It was like becoming a beast of burden.

In a month's time Sharafat developed fever and cough and was forced to give up his work. But he refused to see a doctor. The little money, he had earned, he spent on Sheikhu's meals. But soon that money was also over. The only saleable item which he possessed was a wristwatch. That also went, and could only fetch a couple of more meals for Sheikhu. Then there was all darkness.

One day his sons came back from work and made a suggestion which squeezed the life out of Sharafat. "We heard today that government departments, like Police and Customs, hire horses and dogs to help them with their work. When these animals become old and invalid they are shot. The government doesn't spend on animals who do not work," Yusuf informed.

"Why are you telling me all that, I am not interested in what happens in government departments," Sharafat said with anger.

"*Abba* don't be angry, today by chance, we met a contractor who collects such invalid animals from not only the government departments, but also from private people, and pays a good sum for them." Yusuf said and continued, "Tomorrow he will come and talk to you, if you are satisfied then you can hand over Sheikhu to him."

"Contractor indeed!" Sharafat shouted despite tears in his throat, "Don't dare to call that killer, that murderer to my door. How could you, my son, ever think of making such a suggestion to me," Sharafat was distraught.

"I made this suggestion in Sheikhu's interest, Yunus and I love him as much as you do, *Abba*. We won't be able to see him starving," Yusuf said, and thought his father believed him.

"You don't have faith in Allah? Why would Allah starve some creation of His who had slogged all his life to feed a family of human beings? And don't think I would ever ask any of you to feed me or my wife or my horse," Sharafat shouted and rushed out of his thatched room. He stood in the open and wept inconsolably. Sheikhu who had gone a little distance away to graze on a patch of grass, immediately turned towards their house, and galloped all the way, despite his injury, to where Sharafat stood. He lifted his injured forelegs, touched Sharafat's shoulders with them and started rubbing his mouth against his face. And then he looked right into Sharafat's wet eyes and neighed. He had never neighed like that before. The sound of that neighing pierced through not only Sharafat's heart but the hearts of all those neighbours who had rushed out of their homes to watch a scene drenched in pain and helplessness.

Sharafat felt lighter after having wept and after seeing Sheikhu's reaction. He caressed him and took him to his shed. As he walked to the shed, he shouted again, loud and clear, for his sons to hear. "Allah will send help; He will not be long in sending. He will never let my Sheikhu remain hungry. He will never make me and my Sheikhu depend on others. I have full faith in Allah."

That night Sharafat went to bed on an empty stomach. The small amount of gram which he served to Sheikhu also remained untouched. Both Sharafat and his wife slept in Sheikhu's shed, because he had become suspicious of his sons' designs. Sharafat could never again trust his sons. He had no fears about Sheikhu's meals. He was confident that he would be able to earn enough to feed him. But if he died and Sheikhu lived who'll take care of that poor helpless animal. In the big wide world Sharafat could not think of even one person with whom he could leave Sheikhu. Sharafat couldn't find a moment's sleep. And the night drifted painfully towards dawn.

Sharafat got up, and as usual, took Sheikhu for a walk. That was the vet's advice. The horse had to be kept mobile but was not to carry or pull any weight. A kilometre away was his friend's eatery where he stopped to chat. Sheikhu waited nearby. Sharafat's friend was alone. It was too early for customers to start coming. Sharafat thought it was the right time to ask him for a job. "I know a lot about cooking, which I picked up from the families of the *taluqedars* my father and grandfather served." Sharafat, was not wrong. He made the best *shami kababs* and *parathas*, and his friends had tasted them on many occasions. "I do need some help in the shop. But I may not be able to pay you much, you have a large family to support," his friend replied. "I don't need much; my two sons are independent, my daughters are married; I just need enough to feed Sheikhu and he doesn't eat even half of what he used to; your bhabhi and I will be satisfied if we get some leftovers from the shop," Sharafat said. "This suits me," the friend replied. Just then, they saw two men, perhaps father and son, approaching them from the road. Both of them looked at Sheikhu and asked, "Whose horse is this?"

"Mine *Huzoor*," Sharafat said with pride. The two looked at Sharafat with great interest and the older of the two asked, "Is your name Sharafat Ullah?"

"You are right *Huzoor*. But how do you know the name of your humble servant?" Sharafat asked.

"We sat in your tonga some twenty-six years ago, your name was written on it. You were very young then, we recognised you because of your horse," the older man said.

"*Huzoor*, twenty-six years ago, it was not this horse who pulled my tonga but his mother Gulbadan, This horse was not even born then. But you are right, he looks exactly like his mother; he is much taller, though."

"We recognised him by his pure white face and blackish brown body. This combination of colours on a horse is easy to remember but not all that common," the young man said.

"You know Sharafat Mian, it is not very often that one meets an angel like you, but we have been so unfortunate that we could not even thank you for all that you did for us," the old gentleman said.

"*Huzoor*, what are you saying, I do not understand," Sharafat could really not make out what the father and son wanted to thank him for.

The two men took Sharafat aside and reminded him of a hot day in June 1968, when he had consented to take them to Akbari Gate on his tonga from the clinic of a tuberculosis specialist in Hazratganj. For half an hour, rickshaw pullers and tongawalas had been refusing them. The old man was then about thirty-seven, a poor father of two young boys, one of them so badly consumed with Tuberculosis that he had to be carried by him in his arms. The boys were twins. The sick boy succumbed to his ailment on the way in the tonga, when they were not even half way from the house they wanted to go to. The distraught father was left with no other option but to hide the fact of death of the boy from the tongawala for fear of being told by him to vacate the tonga. The man was aware, that all transport, whether rail or road, was bound either by law or custom, to remove forthwith from the vehicle the dead body of anyone who happened to die on the way. He could not risk the tongawala telling him to get down with the body. He would have had no other option but to beg, on the road, for money, to arrange for a hearse car, to go first to Akbari Gate where his wife was lodged with some relatives, and then, to go back to their home in a village near Sandila from where they had come for their child's treatment. In that moment of tragedy he had to retain his composure and control his tears.

The tongawala reached them without a word to the Akbari Gate house. The father rushed into the house with the body, followed by his son carrying the cloth bag with the medicines. Both broke down, along with the mother. The thought of the tongawala came to the minds of the father and the ten-year-old son when they found a hundred rupee note in the cloth bag. It was stuck to a medicine bottle with a rubber band. The son pointed out to the father that he had first rushed towards the door of the house empty handed, but thought of the bag with the newly bought, and yet unused medicine bottles, and had returned to the tonga to get the bag. The tongawala had handed the bag to him. Both father and son were sure that the tongawala had slipped the hundred rupee note into the bag during that time. Perhaps he had correctly assessed their financial condition! It was indeed that note which had saved them from social disgrace and had made it possible for him to give his child a dignified funeral.

Sharafat wept when he heard the story which he had only partly known and had long forgotten. He wiped his eyes and consoled the father and son for whom that terrible day in June 1968 appeared to have dawned again. He offered them a glass each of sherbet from his friend's dhaba. After giving them directions to his house he requested them to visit him whenever it was convenient for them.

That sad day, long forgotten, came to haunt Sharafat too. Had he not been on his way to buy a new tonga, when hailed by the tragedy stricken father and sons, he would never have been in the possession of a hundred rupee note. He recalled how one look at the helplessness of the threesome made him postpone his journey to the carriage maker's factory. The owner had promised to give him a new tonga in exchange of the old one, plus a hundred rupees. Though a new tonga could come into his life only ten years later, he had never regretted. The incident had never returned to Sharafat's mind again but the moment of death of the sick boy, as seen by him in the mirror before him had remained in his psyche for years. He knew that the boy had died much before the father knew.

He was happy to know that he had made a positive difference to their lives, and was overwhelmed that they had not forgotten him. He became convinced that the world also had good people, not just those who use helpless animals for their benefit and then kill them. In the evening the father and son landed up at Sharafat's humble abode loaded with presents and with *maunds* of gram for Sheikhu. They sat together exchanging notes like old friends. Sharafat was told by the father how times changed for them. After the tragedy, the father, who was a primary school teacher, concentrated on the education of his surviving son. Luckily the son was brilliant. He won scholarships and the attention of a philanthropist who sent him to America to study medicine. He came back to India to a roaring practice and soon built a hospital in Lucknow and one in their village, where the poor were treated free.

The father and son begged Sharafat, but in vain, to accept some money from them to buy a younger horse, or to open an eatery. They could not even convince him to accept some job in their Hospital. "I am totally illiterate what can I do in a hospital?" Sharafat was immensely touched at the eagerness of the father and son to help him out, but he was not willing to take any help from them. "That would amount to my putting a price on the little help which I gave them just by chance. God forbid if I ever help anyone with the expectation of a return," Sharafat thought to himself. He then turned towards the father and said, "*Huzoor* your blessings should remain with me, that is all I want". The old man put his hands on Sharafat's head to bless him and turned to leave. But even before they reached the road where their car was parked, they turned back and were standing again in front of Sharafat, "Can we do something for Sheikhu?" Sharafat's face lit up and he said, "Yes, Doctor Sahib". This time Sharafat was addressing the son. Both father and son looked hopefully at Sharafat. "You are much younger than me, I am sure God will keep you in this world long after I have left. Can you give me your word that you will look after Sheikhu with love and care if I die before him?" The son grabbed Sharafat's hands, kissed them with devotion, then touched them to his eyes and said, "I promise Sharafat *Bhai*, Sheikhu is my child now. God has given me two children earlier; today He has given me a third." Sharafat knew that the young doctor meant what he said.

Sharafat's sons stood nearby watching the scene with mouths wide open. Addressing them Sharafat said, "Did I not say that Allah will send help. He will not be long in sending..."

Nawab Sahib

It is a fine Sunday morning and I am in my Butler Palace Colony flat yet to exercise and bathe. Breakfast will obviously follow later. Kedar, who works for me, suddenly knocks at my door and announces, "Nawab Sahib has come," as though coming of some Nawab Sahib is a normal feature at that hour. "Which Nawab Sahib? From where? For God's sake!" I am irritated.

I soon realise that though my irritation is not uncalled for, my queries are. In Lucknow a nawab doesn't need to be specified. A nawab is a nawab and that is the end of it. There are more possibilities than one, of the nawab being minus estate and minus credentials. In that case, he is referred to as *nawab be mulk* behind his back. In his presence he is showered all the deference which a propertied nawab deserves. So despite my irritation I get up, give myself some time with a comb and mirror and walk into the drawing room.

The man I encounter looks far from a nawab. He is wearing a cheap safari suit, carrying files and speaking Hindi, the type you hear in the corridors of the Uttar Pradesh Secretariat. I am confused. Perhaps there is a mix up. Perhaps, this man's name is Nawab, for in this part of India even that is possible. If you are not born a nawab, then, there are chances of your being named Nawab by your doting parents. In Lucknow and around, you have Nawab Rae, Nawab Singh, Nawab Ali even Nawaboo.

But I am proved wrong. My visitor this morning is a direct descendant of His Majesty King Amjad Ali Shah and his principal consort. He has with him, for my quick reference, his *shijra*, his family tree, in one of those files tucked under his arm. The other files are full of correspondence which he has had with the state government, and also records of his litigation.

He informs me that, after a prolonged litigation, he was declared the rightful owner of Sibtainabad Maqbara and Imambara and the attached property. This Maqbara is the last resting place of King Amjad Ali Shah and is a part of Hazratganj.

"So you are once again a rich man," I say.

"*Alhamdulillah*, may you live long *mohtarma*, your most humble servant will fill your *mubarak* mouth with ghee and sugar if, what your most exalted self says, comes true. But as things are today, and I am thankful to the Almighty even for that, your humble servant is as poor as he was. All this he says not in the lingo of the Secretariat but in the language and style of his forebears.

"Nawab Sahib, it is very kind of you to have come, is there anything specific which I can do for you…how do you know me." At last I stammer out some questions to find out what exactly he wants from me, and who he is, after all.

"Is there any one in Lucknow, *gharibparvar*, who does not know your most respected and dignified self. The fragrance of your personality has travelled far and wide, *gharib nawaz*. Your heart is like wax. It melts to see an ant in pain. Your most humble *ghulam*, has come with great hopes," he stops and looks beseechingly at me. I wish he would go on. It feels great hearing all that about oneself.

"Tell me how I can help you Nawab Sahib," I know I am asking for trouble, and yet I want to help him. I must admit I feel quite obliged to him for making that flattering little speech in my honour.

"*Mohtarma*," Nawab Sahib says, "I am a poor man without resources and without connections. The Lucknow Development Authority was the owner of Sibtainabad Maqbara till now. If they make it difficult for me to take over the title of the property, I will be able to do nothing, to help myself. Your great self is so high in the government. Can you not use your influence to put in a word for me?" This time he is forthright. Had he beaten about the bush, I could have easily got away with a bureaucratic reply. I didn't know a soul in the Lucknow Development Authority. I begin fumbling for a reply. Just then Kedar walks in, like a saviour, and announces breakfast.

I invite Nawab Sahib to share the morning meal with me, but my offer is very politely turned down by him. After great persuasion he agrees to have a cup of tea, which he holds in great style between his fingers. He barely sips the tea, just touches his lips to the cup, uses beautiful language to praise it, and showers blessings on me, "*Jeeti rahiye khush rahiye.*" All my powers of persuasion fail to coax him into tasting anything else. He appears too satiated to be tempted.

My inclination to help him increases. This man who has spent half his life knocking at the gates of the judiciary with no resources, deserves a push. He must have spent a hell of a lot of money. Where did he get all that money from? I am curious, but reluctant to ask. Instead I ask him his address.

"*Rehne deejye, mohtarma*," he says, "I have no address. I am a poor man, I'll come again myself." I do not insist. He leaves after an elaborate farewell.

Another Sunday dawns and before the June sun can play havoc with it, Nawab Sahib is knocking at my door again. This time he has books in his hands instead of files.

"Last time I noticed that you are interested in the *Nawabi* period of Lucknow's history. Perhaps these books can be of some help." The books, which he spreads on the table before me, are some very rare books on the city.

"When may I return them and where?" I ask. I am really happy to get them.

"How long would you take to read them, *mohtarma*?"

"A month."

"You can keep them for a lifetime if you so wish," he says with the generosity one expects of a Nawab.

"A lifetime is not necessary, a month will do," I laugh light-heartedly.

"I will come again on a Sunday like this, after a month."

"Nawab Sahib, I am putting you to too much trouble. Allow me to bring the books back to you."

"No trouble at all *mohtarma*, it will be a pleasure," he says not eager to stretch the subject, and leaves.

It is more than three months and Nawab Sahib has not come for his books. I make enquiries about the Nawab. A lot of people know him, but no one knows where exactly he lives. At last an idea strikes me. The *Wasiqa* office! That is where the descendants of the rulers of Awadh get their pension. That's where I can get his whereabouts. I am right. The office enlightens me about his address. He lives near Kazman. I rush in that direction and park the car near the side gate of Kazman. An urchin reaches me to his house, a dilapidated little structure with crumbling walls. A sackcloth hanging over the door. From a hole in this curtain the begum informs me that Nawab Sahib had gone for work.

The same urchin leads me on to the Nawab's place of work and tells me on the way that he is a *zardozi karigar*, and works for someone who owns a factory. When we reach the factory the little boy points his finger towards a small house. I stand at a distance and look in that direction. It takes me no time to spot the Nawab, although he is not in the attire I saw him in. A *tehmad* is wrapped round his waist and there is no shirt on his back. He is bent over a wooden frame, an *adda* across which is stretched yards of maroon velvet. A number of other workers, including children, are bent similarly over the cloth. His bare back shines with sweat as his deft fingers pull out the needle from the cloth leaving behind a trail of gold. Nawab Sahib is conscious of nothing except that gold on the cloth. I decide not to disturb this determined and dedicated son of the kings. I am confident, he will return to my flat, one Sunday morning, to take back his books and, may be, to find out whether I have spoken to someone who can help him to get back the property of his ancestors.

Autumn Leaves and Calvary[*]

Angela is Five
Angela suddenly left my index finger and ran towards the falling leaf. She wanted to catch it before it touched the earth and when she could not, she just stood by and watched it fall. It was a shrivelled, dried up leaf with no traces of chlorophyll in it. The moment it fell, the wind swept it away along with so many other dead leaves. Angela lost sight of it. She looked around for a moment, and then turned to me.

"Mama, why wasn't there a noise when the leaf fell on the ground, and there were so many of them which fell and none of them made a noise. Why don't leaves make a noise when they fall? Tell me Mama."

"They do, but autumn leaves do not," I told her.

"But why?" As a child Angela was generally quiet but she was curious about strange things. Her curiosity about autumn leaves was not to be quenched easily, but I tried to explain, "By the time autumn comes the tree refuses to give food to the leaves, so they become weak and sick and one day, they die and quietly fall off."

---

[*]   This story appeared in the *Hindustan Times* Sunday Weekly on 3 May 1980.

"Naughty tree," Angela's eyes flashed with anger, "but why don't they beat the tree?"

"Because, the tree is bigger."

"Then why don't they cry?"

"They know the tree would not listen to them."

"Then why don't they tell God about the dirty tree?"

"That would not help them either, my pet."

"Even God can't help the poor autumn leaves?" Angela's eyes widened with surprise and her voice choked with emotion.

"When you start going to school darling, you will get books and teachers who will tell you all about trees and flowers and autumn leaves."

"But no one will ever tell me why autumn leaves don't make a noise when they fall," Angela stamped her tiny foot with anger.

"But you will know it," I said and collected that angry little bundle into my arms and rushed into the house.

Angela is Eight

Grace over. We sat down to eat. Angela refused to touch the food.

"Now little one, you won't eat this lovely jalebi pudding which mama made for you," I said, forcing a spoonful of pudding into Angela's mouth.

"No I don't want to eat jalebi pudding; I want to know how far is Calvary."

We were surprised. We guessed of course, that Angela had been told something regarding Christ's crucifixion in school, but none of us were prepared for this query.

"How far from where, darling?" Albert, Angela's father, wanted to know what was going on in her mind.

"From where Jesus had to carry the Cross on his shoulders," Angela asked.

Her mind was still not clear to us. We paused for a while for we did not know what answer would satisfy her.

"Calvary is the place where they nailed our Lord to the Cross and left him on it till he died," Albert was still groping in the dark.

"I know that Daddy, and that Cross was very heavy and still He had to carry it on his poor shoulders all the way to Calvary. I wonder for how long he had to carry it?" Angela was almost in tears.

"Not for very long," I tried to calm her down.

"But for how long?"

I persuaded her to get into bed and bribed her into sleep. I always did that when I found myself unable to answer her questions.

Angela is Twenty-two

Angela had lived up to our expectations. She completed her studies with a first division in biochemistry and topped the Lucknow University. This was sure to get her a good job in the university or in a research institute. That was a lucky year in other respects too. The summer holidays brought me a number of tuitions. Even Angela gave music lessons to two rich girls. Since Albert lost his job with the local newspaper, money came into our house only sporadically and in very small quantities. I wonder what we would have done without the extra money that summer. My mother was visiting us with my brother's family for the first time since they left for England just before Independence. Eighteen summers had gone by while I longed to be near my dear ones, but financial problems and responsibility of the house never allowed a meeting. It was ecstasy to be with mother once again. But it was more than that to see my nephew Denzil's eyes, each time Angela was around. They followed her wherever she went. My house echoed with their laughter, and for the first time I saw roses on Angela's cheeks. It was my turn now to ask Angela "Why do roses bloom?" Just as she asked me all those questions as a child. But before I could ask her, they had already faded and then withered. For two months after my folks left, I used to see a Khakhi clad postman hand over letters to Angela more frequently than he ever did before. And then he stopped coming. A couple of months later, he appeared again, and this time he brought a letter for me. It was from Dick, my brother. He had asked me to advise Angela to desist from writing to Denzil. I was also informed of Denzil's engagement to an English girl of a "suitable background". They were to be married before Easter. I said nothing to Angela but I left the letter on the piano. I don't even know whether she read it; but I know for sure those roses never bloomed again on her cheek, not even when she got the job, she aspired for, in The Central Drug Research Institute; not even when she got a national award for her research in drugs. And as years rolled by Angela's research in her subject brought recognition for her and glory for us. How I wished I could exchange all that glory for roses, roses that I wanted to see blossoming from my child's face.

Angela is Thirty-one: The First Christmas in Delhi
And then Angela got that coveted assignment in Delhi; she left Lucknow, while we stayed behind only to visit her in Christmas.

And at Christmas we saw in Angela a totally different person. She was radiating good health. Joy oozed out of every pore of her body. I had never seen Angela so happy, not even during that brief summer when my folks had visited us from England. Her job was satisfying, her bosses kind and her colleagues very helpful. In fact one of her colleagues we met on the very first day. He landed at her apartment with a bouquet of fresh flowers and placed them, in my hands, "To welcome you, Mama." I admit I was taken aback at the warm reception.

He was a man of Angela's age, perhaps slightly older, with a receding hairline, a friendly grin revealing a set of uneven liberally spaced teeth. There was something about his face which made people laugh, while he himself carried an amused expression in his eyes. In the one month that we spent in Delhi we saw a lot of him. He spent practically all his waking hours with Angela in her apartment. I took no time to realise that he was more than a colleague for her. He was fast taking over whatever hold Albert and her three brothers and I had on her. The relationship seemed to grow with each day that went. At least it appeared so to me, till I heard from Angela that he was a married man and in three months time was to become a father. When Angela met him two months ago, his wife, the daughter of a very highly placed man, was already four months pregnant. This information numbed my senses.

I stood up in despair and shook Angela by the shoulders. I wanted to warn her, I wanted to pull her away from the tip of the precipice she was standing upon. But I could do nothing. Angela looked at me with her large hazel eyes. There was hope and trust pouring out from them.

"Mama," she said, "he is not happy with his wife, he proposes to take a divorce from her." Angela thought those words would drug me just as they had drugged her.

It was with a very heavy heart that I left Delhi for Lucknow.

The Second Christmas in Delhi

Angela's apartment was as cheerful as Angela herself. Angela's colleague welcomed us again with a friendly grin and a bouquet of fresh flowers. Throughout the month that I was there, I heard her flat echoing with laughter and music. But the news I wanted to hear did not come and soon the time arrived for me to leave for Lucknow.

The Third Christmas in Delhi

Everything was as before, including the bouquet of flowers and the friendly grin. I managed to find time alone with Angela.

"What happened to his plans?" I asked.

"He has not been able to speak to his wife, his child has not been keeping well," I saw an element of fear creeping into Angela's eyes. "He will speak to her as soon as the child is well." Angela brought hope into her voice, but could do nothing to hide that streak of fear in her eyes.

The Fourth Christmas in Delhi

Nothing had changed. All was as before including the bouquet of flowers and the amused eyes behind them.

"What is the progress my child?" This was me, anxiety-driven, addressing Angela.

"Mama, he has an unmarried sister, he does not want to start the legal proceedings till she gets married." And soon the sister too got married, but the fifth Christmas came and went, and so did the sixth leaving behind nothing for Angela, but stealing away the bloom from her cheeks. And this time when I met her even the facade of hope in her eyes had disappeared and I saw naked despair glaring at me from her eyes.

Angela is Thirty-seven
"What are you waiting for little one?" I asked.

"For Calvary Mama," I heard Angela's frail voice.

I became wild at my child's sufferings. "Oh Angela you cannot let him get away like this, you must force him to keep his promise."

"The weak cannot use force on the strong, Mama," Angela sighed.

"How can you call yourself weak with all your achievements, your qualifications, your success?"

"Achievements and qualifications don't make a person strong, Mama."

"But remaining quiet would not help, you must tell his parents, his wife, his top-shot father-in-law. You must get justice, he cannot just back out after six long years. Had you been a girl from any other place than Lucknow, I am sure, you would not have allowed that scoundrel to get away unpunished. He has taken advantage of your *tehzeeb* and your inborn decency."

"Making a noise would not help Mama," Angela said.

"Oh Darling, at least pray to God to help you," I was desperate.

"Mama, I do not think even God can help."

"Why can't God help, He can always help, my child."

"Not after the approach of autumn, Mama." And Angela, drained of all hope and cheer, looked as lifeless as an autumn leaf ready to fall.

"But my child ..." I tried to reason with Angela.

Angela stopped me midway.

"Dear Mama, I am tired of answering your questions. Why don't you answer mine, like old times. I have been carrying my cross for too long Mama, tell me how far is Calvary?" Angela had given me almost three decades to answer this question and I still did not know the answer. All that I knew was that the cross Angela was carrying was too heavy, and that there were no short cuts to Calvary.

Zulekha

"Raja Sahib, how can you think of marrying my nephew's wife? My real brother's son's wife?" Zaibun's world was spinning round her.

"Why can't I?" Raja Badaruzzaman of Surajpur put a counter question so casually that Zaibun almost lost her mind.

"Your wife's nephew is your nephew, you can't marry your nephew's wife," Zaibun explained referring to the rules of the religion which both of them professed.

"My wife's nephew? Shehzad is not my wife's nephew," Raja Sahib's answer was cryptic. Blunt and point-blank.

"Isn't he my nephew?" Zaibun asked.

"Yes he is; but you are not my wife," the raja made that statement with no hesitation and Zaibun's world came crashing down. She stood speechless for some time, and then, with great difficulty, found words to ask him, "Haven't we been married for fifteen long years and living together most happily? Our *nikah* was celebrated in this very house. Wasn't it?"

"Zaibunnisa Begum," the raja called her by her name for the first time, "I have been wanting for a long time to explain to you, but could not bring myself to do it."

"To do what?" Zaibun was in a state of frenzy.

"To tell you that the *nikah*, which was performed to solemnise our marriage, was a totally fake one. The qazi was fake, the witnesses were fake. It was actually no *nikah*," The *taluqedar* of Surajpur was sitting on Zaibun's bed while making that nerve-racking statement.

Zaibun asked no more questions. She just got up, pulled him by the hand and pushed him out of the room. "You tell me that our *nikah* was a fake one and continue to sit on my bed. You don't have the right to even look at my face. Get out this minute, you master of crime, and never be seen anywhere near my house, I don't even care to ask you why you organised that fake *nikah*."

"But I will tell you why. You insisted that you'll have nothing to do with me until I married you. I was too much in love with you to let you go. You were not prepared to settle down with me as a mistress. And I was too weak to go against the norms of society," Raja Sahib explained.

"Strange explanation! You cheated me because you loved me," she said, and broke down. The heart breaking revelations of the day left her mind in a kind of vacuum. There was a hollow feeling within her and yet her whole body trembled ceaselessly with the aftershock of the raja's confessions. She could not think straight.

There had been events in her life, earlier too, which had shaken her existence and numbed her senses; like that terrible morning during the plague epidemic in her village, when she woke up to find both her parents dead, her dear brother Sajjad, a two year old, sucking at his dead mother's breasts. In her village people were lying in the throes of death like flies collapsing after a rain of pesticides. There was no one left in the vicinity that could come to her rescue. Again that ugly evening when she realised that the woman that she was working for as a kitchen maid was actually a *tawaif*, whose intentions were not honourable. And finally, that dark night when she too joined the world of *tawaifs* at the age of thirteen and was rechristened Zulekha. All these incidents had shattered her dreams, no doubt, but had kept her hopes alive and her determination on fire, to make the best of her life and that of her brother. But her husband's deceit which was unveiled today took away her trust from all human beings.

For days her mind did not settle into the present time frame. She looked into the past for reasons as to why the Raja stooped to the depths which he did. She found none. Horror and tragedy had confronted her from childhood. She was surrounded by cruel, dishonest and deceptive people. But she found none falling so low. Even Naseeban Bai, the ageing courtesan she worked for as a kitchen maid, and who had forced her to become a *tawaif*, had reasons of her own for doing so. Naseeban Bai's resources were fast running out and, at her age, she could not hope to earn much from the profession she was in. She had every reason to see, in the beautiful ten-year old orphan girl, who had accidentally landed at her house, a future source of income. If Naseeban trained her in song and dance and introduced her into her profession, she was doing something she needed to do.

Zaibun's two unsuccessful efforts to run away from Naseeban's *kotha* had earned her severe beatings. When

Naseeban had beaten her blue and black, the second time, she made Zaibun sit in front of her for a question-answer session.

"Look Zaibun, I am sorry for the terrible pain caused to you. Since you made desperate efforts twice to leave my house, you must be having a place to go to. I want to know where that is, so that I make arrangements to leave you and your brother there."

Zaibun looked at her with disbelief and then with horror.

"I am asking you a very simple question. If you tell me the place, and the name of the people you want to go to, I will drop you there. If a girl of your age makes the effort herself with a little baby in her lap she may fall into worse hands than mine." And Zaibun realised the folly of her effort. "Where was I running away to?" Zaibun asked herself. "I have no one I can go to, I know not a place, where I can find refuge!" And that was the moment she made peace with herself and promised to obey Naseeban. Another reason which gave strength to her decision was that Naseeban was never cruel to her brother Sajjad. Strangely enough he was fast becoming the apple of her eye.

And so at the age of thirteen, after a brief "*nath uthrai*" ceremony Naseeban Bai initiated Zaibun into her profession. "You will be called Zulekha from today. Zaibun is not a name for beautiful women. Throw that name out from your system, only then you will be able to put a lid on other unhappy memories," Naseeban Bai advised.

Zaibun could neither throw out from her system the name by which her parents called her, nor could she put a lid on her memories. And yet she resolved to reach the top and leave all other women of her adopted profession behind.

Naseeban Bai lived just for five years after initiating Zaibun into her profession. For those five years Zaibun was given no right to spend her earnings as she liked. But Naseeban imposed no restriction on the money spent on Sajjad's education. Zaibun wanted nothing more.

At eighteen Zulekha was her own boss. By then her name was established and she had picked up not only the tricks of the trade but also the rules. She knew that if her beauty was important for her success her talent was even more important. And for that her *ustad* was never to be dispensed and her *riyaz* was to be adhered to most religiously. Zulekha's priorities were right. In a few years she was the top *tawaif* of Lucknow, much loved and much in demand. For the next twenty years Zulekha ruled over the hearts of Lucknow aristocrats, with her ethereal beauty, her golden voice and her command over the Kathak dance form. No other *tawaif* could match her talents.

Success and hard work did not take away Zulekha's attention from her brother. She knew that her father was an educated person, though it was in a very small village school that he taught Arabic and Persian. She wanted Sajjad to get the highest education in those languages. By the time he was twelve, she shifted him into the most prestigious school of theology which was Lucknow's pride. By the age of twenty Sajjad was teaching in the same school. It was then that Zulekha asked him to revive touch with their village. He found a few survivors of the plague, who remembered his father and family. That re-established his respectability. The villagers took him as the sole survivor in that family and believed him when he told them that a God-fearing woman who lived in Lucknow brought him up and educated him. The reunion with people of his village helped Sajjad to marry Jamila from a respectable family of the area. Though, in course of time, his wife discovered the truth about his sister. She kept it all to herself.

"The fact remains that you belong to a respectable family of that village. Your sister had no other alternative, I can understand," Jamila said to Sajjad when she learnt the truth.

"At that time, what a problem I must have been for a ten year old child. But my sister never thought so. I was her first priority," Sajjad reflected on the situation in retrospect.

"Another child of ten would have abandoned a two year old sibling," Jamila's respect for Sajjad's sister had gone up. "But how did you reach the *tawaif's* house?"

"In the village, there was no one to give us refuge. An English padre took us with him. My sister worked as a cleaning maid in their house. The padre's wife allowed her to keep me with her inside the house. My sister thought they were a nice couple. But their khansama who was also a Muslim, became overprotective. He thought their intentions were to convert us to Christianity."

"Oh no, was it he who took the two of you to Lucknow to that *tawaif*?"

"Yes him and the ayah of the family. But my sister believes that their intentions were good and they had no idea that Naseeban was a *tawaif*."

Jamila took a deep breath, and said, "That is what you call destiny." Jamila proved to be an understanding and loving wife. Sajjad's life started on a happy note. Zulekha had striven for just that. At last she felt that she had won the respectability, at least for her brother, which had slipped out of her hands. She resolved to keep away from Sajjad and his family as far as possible.

But this happy arrangement went on only for eight years. The couple had three children. At the third child's birth Jamila died. The child, a daughter, survived. Poor Zulekha had to enter the scene again. And worse was to follow. Sajjad could not pull on without Jamila for long. He also died within a few years leaving his three children as orphans.

During his last days, he would hold on to his sister's hand and apologise, "*Baji Amma*, I have always been the cause of tension for you."

"What are you saying my child. On the contrary, you have always been the cause of my happiness. You have brought joy and fulfilment into my life," Zulekha said.

"Earlier you had one child to worry about. Now I am leaving three children to your care," Sajjad sounded so helpless.

Zulekha put her fingers on his lips, swallowed her tears and said, "Never talk of leaving *Beta*; never utter such unhappy words. You are not my brother, you are my child. I would have killed myself had God not given you to me."

But it was only for a short time that God had given Sajjad to her. He took him away when he was needed most. Zulekha was devastated. For months there was no sound from her *kotha*. And yet Zulekha had to get up again, put aside her personal loss and forget about her pain. It was the suffering of the three motherless and fatherless children that became her supreme concern. She expanded her house, built a portion for the children, which was totally cut off from the *nashist gah* where she performed and entertained. She did not want the children to have anything to do with that part of the house. She protected and guarded the children jealously and kept them away from even herself. As soon as they were of age she put them in a good boarding school, she wanted them to face the world with the relevant education of the times and not have even the faintest knowledge of their aunt's profession.

To support all that Zulekha needed to reopen her *kotha*, and rejuvenate herself. And rejuvenate herself she did. This new phase of her life shone brighter than ever before. It was around this time that she met Raja Badaruzzaman of Surajpur at a *mehfil* organised by another *taluqedar* of Awadh for his son's wedding. Zulekha's Kathak performance at that function became a legend. She created magic through her excellent footwork. Her control on the sound of the *ghungroos* and the thirty-six different facial expressions she gave to depict a single couplet of Ghalib, mesmerised the audience. It was Zulekha's evening. She returned to her *kotha* not just many times richer but as the creator of a legendary moment in the cultural history of Lucknow. And Raja Badaruzzaman went back home besotted by her.

A colourful courtship followed but there was no proposal for marriage. This was quite normal. *taluqedar*s or anyone from good families would seldom marry a *tawaif*. Though there were many who kept them as mistresses. The Raja was already married and had grown up children. Yet he spent most of his time with her. He offered her half his property and an attractive monthly allowance and requested her to live with him. Zulekha refused to have anything to do with him until he married her. For Zulekha, to be someone's mistress was as degrading as to be a *tawaif*. It was not property or money that she needed. That she had in plenty. As a *tawaif* too, Zulekha's earnings were the envy of many a rich people of Lucknow. She was among the first few residents of the city who owned a car. The house she lived in, as a *tawaif*, could easily be put in the category of houses owned by nawabs and *taluqedar*s. She lived like a rani earlier too, but she yearned for the respectability she had lost. She longed to be someone's wife. She wanted acceptability in society for herself and for Sajjad's children. She wanted them to have a normal family life like she had, before the plague took her parents away. She did not want them to grow up trying to hide their relationship with her.

At last the raja consented. The *nikah* took place in one of his houses in Lucknow in the presence of four men, two of whom were his servants.

After this marriage, Zulekha felt that all her dreams had turned into reality. The raja treated her with love and respect. He gave Sajjad's children the affection which children need and when they reached marriageable age he helped her to marry them off in good families. But Zulekha saw to it that she spent her own money on their education and for settling them down.

"It is just my humble request Raja Sahib," Zulekha had told the Raja right in the beginning, "There is no difference between your money and mine, but you should let me spend on the education and bringing up of Sajjad's children, from what little money I have."

Raja Sahib insisted on bearing the expenses himself.

"Raja Sahib, it is you who are looking after them. Your presence and your protection, means a lot for them. Since there is a little money with me why stack it away," Zulekha used the softest possible words to make her point.

"No," the raja insisted.

Zulekha did not give up. "You had told me once that you want all three sons of yours to go to Cambridge University in *Vilayat*. So far only one is studying there. Isn't it time now for the other two to follow him?"

The raja became thoughtful, and Zulekha continued, "I know they are your sons, not mine. But you don't realise how proud I will be when all three come back to India after studying in *Vilayat*. Don't take from me that privilege." And the Raja Sahib gave in.

Sajjad's children did well, like their father. The eldest, Shehzad, wrote poetry in Urdu. He was considered a good poet. He became known all over India. Some of his *ghazals* became hit songs in the Bombay film industry in the early forties. Buniyad took his father's and grandfather's profession and became a teacher in Lucknow's famous school of theology. Amina was married to a young man who had set up a shoe factory.

Things looked fine for once. Zulekha was happy. She thought that her past had been erased from her life, but she didn't realise that a *tawaif's* past remains plastered on her life forever, neither did she suspect that her biggest heartbreak was yet to come. She never imagined in her wildest of dreams that after a decade and a half of a happy "married life", the man she thought was her husband will walk in, as casually as ever, one day, and disclose, that she was never his wife because the *nikah* was never a real one; that he was going to marry someone else, her own nephew's wife, young enough to be his granddaughter!

And how could she have imagined all that, when for the entire period that man had given her all that she could have asked for.

It is true that Zulekha had noticed for some time that things were not fine between Shehzad and his wife Kaneez Fatima, but she did not realise that it would take away her dear nephew's happiness and throw a dark shadow on her life too.

One day when she was sitting in her lawn enjoying a glass of sherbet with the raja, a maid announced that Kaneez Fatima's mother wanted to see him. The lady was called with all respect and offered a chair and a glass of sherbet.

"*Adab Arz* Begum Sahib. I hope all is fine at home."

"Yes Raja Sahib, all is fine in my home but not here," Kaneez's mother said.

"God forbid, has anything gone wrong?" Zulekha asked.

"I am addressing Raja Sahib, let him talk to me," her tone was harsh and disrespectful.

"*Farmaiye* Begum Sahib, I am listening," the raja said.

"You have misled us; you kept the truth from us, and persuaded us to marry our daughter to this lady's nephew," Kaneez's mother said with all the harshness she could gather.

"What truth could I have concealed? Shahzad is such a good boy; he is respected and known all over India for his poetry," Raja Sahib said.

"We did not marry our daughter to Shehzad's poetry. We married her to him, imagining that he is from a good family, because you brought the proposal, and you said that he is your *aziz*," she said.

"But this does not mean, that I misled you," Raja Sahib replied.

"You should have told us that he is your second wife's nephew, who is a *tawaif*." Kaneez Fatima's mother said that not just frankly but with all the cruelty she could bring into her voice.

The Raja Sahib looked embarrassed but said nothing.

"I want *talaq* for my daughter," the lady was almost threatening, "although, she'll never be able to get married again. You have, I am sorry to say, spoilt my daughter's life," she said and left.

That exchange of conversation between Shehzad's mother-in-law and Raja Sahib shattered both Zulekha and the Raja Sahib, but for different reasons. Zulekha thought the respectability which she had regained was only an illusion. And Raja Sahib held himself responsible for spoiling the life of a girl from a good family. He saw a point in what the mother said. He agreed that it would not be easy for her to get married again in a respectable family. Perhaps in a state of extreme remorse he thought he could offer his hand in marriage to the girl.

For days an uncomfortable atmosphere prevailed in the house. A few days later Raja Sahib said that he was going to Surajpur. Normally Zulekha accompanied him.

"I'll pack a few clothes and be ready in no time," she told the Raja.

"You don't bother to come, I'll be back very soon," Raja Sahib replied, without looking at her, and left.

He did come back very soon indeed. But he came back to drop the bombshell on her. Her nephews and niece blamed Kaneez Fatima and her mother for what happened. But that was not relevant for Zulekha. What was significant was that her own husband had said that their *nikah* was fake. In that case, their marriage no matter how long it had lasted and how well it had lasted, was no marriage. It was an invalid union. Zulekha remembered that the house she was living in was given to her by Raja Sahib as her '*meher*'. But if there was no *nikah*, there was no *meher*. She returned the legal papers of the house to the Raja and left, with only her personal possessions, to her own house where she earlier lived and entertained as Zulekha *tawaif*. Never again did she have anything to do with Raja Badaruzzaman of Surajpur.

Her nephews Shahzad and Buniyad and her niece Amina rushed after her to that house to bring her back. Each one begged her to stay with them. "*Phuphi Amma* you can't stay in this house. You will be all alone. You stay with one of us, but we will not let you come back to this place," Shahzad said. But Zulekha refused.

"My dear children, who can be dearer to me than you, but I will not stay with any of you. My proximity to you will only harm you."

"*Phuphi Amma* you have brought us up. You are our mother and father both. Your closeness to us can never harm us," Buniyad said, his throat choked with tears and Amina fell crying on her lap. But this time Zulekha was adamant.

"I'll be a fool if even now I do not realise that a *tawaif* will remain a *tawaif*, an outcast, a leper, an untouchable for the rest of society. I am an old woman now, I'll be a fool if after all that has happened, I still hanker after respectability for myself. But yes, I have to see that all is not lost for you. Not much of my life is left. When my Creator beckons me, no one from here will feel ashamed to arrange for my last journey. They will be happy to lend their shoulders to carry me to my grave." It was late evening; time for *maghrib namaz*. Zulekha got up, stretched her right hand and placed it, one by one, on each of her dear children's heads and said, "Now go, I place you under the care of Allah." And as they left she unrolled her *janamaz*, and faced the west, to say her namaz.

Destiny has its Reasons

Faqir Mohammad Khan was a general and at one time the commander-in-chief of the nawab of Awadh's army. He was a Yusufzai Pathan whose ancestors had settled in Malihabad. Huge stretches of lands in Lucknow were also owned by him and were named after him. The most famous were the two large compounds separated by the beautiful British cemetery where lay buried Sir John Collins, resident in the court of Nawab Vazir Sadat Ali Khan of Awadh. The compound facing Moulviganj and touching Aminuddaulah Park from one side was registered as Hata-e-Kham Faqir Mohammad Khan in the municipal records and the one on the other side of the cemetery where stood Jhau Lal's haveli was called Hata-e-Pukhta Faqir Mohammad Khan. To the common man who lived there they were Kachcha Hata and Pucca Hata.

By the 20s of the 20th century there were two schools, one for boys and another for girls, which stood opposite each other on the Moulviganj Road. The rear wall of the boys' school was in Kachcha Hata. Facing this wall were a row of houses some small, some big, some very big, all single storeyed, with terraces joined to each other. The terraces served as socialising venues for the women, kite flying platforms for young boys and once in a while as a secret meeting place for young romancing couples.

Most of the families who lived in these houses were related to each other and those who were not, were known to each other for so long that they were as good as relatives. The story which I am going to tell is not about Faqir Mohammad Khan nor about his times but about Yameen and Saira who lived in two of the very big houses facing the rear wall of the boys' school in Kachcha Hata or Hata-e-Kham Faqir Mohammad Khan as entered in government records and as known in the postal department. The times were those when India was still not partitioned.

Sometimes towards the end of 1946 Yameen qualified for the Central Secretariat Service. No one was happy because this meant that Yameen would have to leave Lucknow and go to Delhi. There were no transfers in the service. The Central Secretariat meant Delhi and only Delhi.

"No one in my family has left Lucknow just for a job," Yameen's mother Rehmatunnisa commented. Yameen's father, Usman, who was in two minds decided to consult a few people before he gave permission to Yameen to take up the job. One was his younger brother Asghar, an advocate, and the other was his boss, the city magistrate, who was an Englishman. Both spoke approvingly of the service.

"Yameen would start on a gazetted class-II post. That is a fairly high position. Remember Mr Usman, you are fifty years old and still a head clerk," the city magistrate said to Usman whom he held in a very high esteem. And Asghar told Usman, "*Bhaijan*, it is a matter of great pride for us that Yameen will begin his career as a gazetted officer. By the time he retires he may be secretary to the Government of India! After hearing both the men whose opinion mattered most to him, Usman was no longer in two minds. That evening, after coming back from office he called Yameen and said, "Yameen my child, I think, you should go to Delhi and take up the job."

"*Abba*, once I take up the Central Secretariat job, I'll be forever cut off from Lucknow," Yameen was almost in tears.

"*Beta*, you will be a gazetted officer at twenty-four, you can't imagine how far you'll go by the time you retire. You'll be well placed money-wise too. Coming to Lucknow for you would be like going to Aminabad Park from Kachcha Hata!"

Rehmatunnisa was not impressed with this logic, nor was Usman's sister Ayesha.

"Yameen has been teaching in Islamia College ever since he did his MA. What's wrong with that? I think the salary is good enough." Rehmatunnisa said. And Ayesha agreed.

"Begum, try to understand. Yameen will be holding a position which the *angrez* holds." Then Usman turned towards his son and asked, "*Beta*, haven't you also appeared for some interview for a post in the United Provinces Secretariat?"

"Yes *Abba*, I appeared for an interview for the U. P. Secretariat job much before the Central Secretariat. But still there is no news about the results." Yameen expressed his concern.

"Don't worry, sooner or later the results will be out. And I am sure they will be in your favour. You can then leave the Delhi job and take up the Lucknow one." Turning to his wife, Usman said, "So Begum, don't worry, it won't be long before Yameen comes back to Lucknow and will be living in this very Kachcha Hata."

The following Sunday Yameen left for Delhi. His mother, sisters, aunts and female cousins walked him till the *mardana* part, the strictly male territory, of the house. His father, uncles, male cousins and many *mohalla* friends accompanied him till Charbagh railway station. As Yameen stepped on the waiting tonga he lifted his eyes towards the sprawling terrace of his house. For a split second he saw a pair of tear-soaked eyes and then the vision disappeared. All that remained was the *anchal* of a multicoloured crinkled *dupatta* which also vanished in the next second. But that split second was enough for tearing to pieces Yameen's heart. Those tear-soaked eyes were those of Saira, his neighbour Moulvi Aijaz Ahmad's daughter, to whom Yameen had got married a month ago. But only the *nikah* had been performed. The *rukhsati* had been postponed till Id. Moulvi Sahib wanted a glamorous wedding for his only child. At the time of the *nikah* he was a little short of money. By Id, a big amount of money was likely to be in his hands from his Zamidari in Pali, District Hardoi. The postponement suited Usman too, for by then he was hopeful to find a groom for one of his five daughters. He would get her married and throw a combined feast for his daughter's wedding and his son's *walima*.

Saira and Yameen's parents were not only neighbours but very good friends. When Saira's mother was pregnant with Saira, Yameen's mother, Rehmatunnisa, said to her, "If you have a daughter, promise that you will marry her to my son Yameen."

"I promise," Saira's mother said. That's how Saira was engaged to Yameen from the time of her birth. This kind of engagement was nothing new to Lucknow. It was a common feature in those times. But in this case Saira and Yameen were also madly in love with each other.

Yameen joined his new service and took a private house in Ballimaran. He was happy with the job because it brought him a high status and a good salary, but his heart was waiting to hear about the U. P. Secretariat job. He wanted to be in Lucknow, so that he was not away from Saira even for a day. But instead of any happy news from the U.P. Secretariat, Yameen got a telegram that his father had suffered a paralytic stroke. He rushed to Lucknow and called the best doctors to treat him. But all was over on the third day of Id. Hectic preparations were going on, in both the families, for Saira's *rukhsati*, but Usman's illness and death brought everything to a standstill, and the *rukhsati* was postponed once again. Usman's death was a great tragedy for his family. He was just fifty years of age. Yameen, at twenty-four, was his eldest child. His widow was left with five unmarried daughters. And yet she was convinced that Saira's *rukhsati* should not be further delayed. Yameen left for Delhi after performing his father's *chaliswan*. But before he left it was decided that Saira's *rukhsati* would take place exactly a month later. This gave some cause of happiness to Yameen. On reaching Delhi he informed his boss that he would require some leave again a month later.

But 1947 had moved far ahead, almost towards mid August. Riots had started in Delhi. Soon they were raging in all parts of the Old City. Muslims were not safe. The postal system too was breaking down. Yameen stopped getting letters from his mother and sisters. His sister Zahra's envelope would carry Saira's letter too. Then came a time when all Muslim government officials were removed, for their safety, from their homes to the Purana Qila, which was guarded by the Army and the Police.

In Lucknow, there was no news of Yameen for more than a month. Newspapers carried details of killings of Muslims in Delhi. His family feared the worst. But by the end of November news came from Yameen's office that he had been evacuated from the Purana Qila and flown to Karachi because he had opted to live and work in Pakistan. There were directions for his family too. His mother, his wife and his five sisters were to leave for Lahore by a train leaving Lucknow on the 16th of December 1947. The train would run under army protection.

"Pakistan?" roared Moulvi Aijaz Ahmad, "What is Pakistan?" He asked.

No one could answer that question, at least not Rehmatunnisa, who had gone to Moulvi Sahib's house to tell him whatever she knew of Yameen's movements, his plans and intentions. She was in a daze herself. She knew not how she would wind up and vacate that huge house which was theirs' for generations, and carry her five young daughters, and one daughter-in-law to a strange place called Pakistan. She had never lived in any other place except Kachcha Hata.

"And how do you know Yameen's intentions and plans?" Moulvi Sahib asked with the same anger in his voice.

"Yameen has sent two letters, one to me and one to Saira through his Delhi office. He had written them before he was flown to Pakistan," Rehmatunnisa said as calmly as she could.

"A letter to Saira, under what right has he written it to her?" Moulvi Sahib asked with authority in his voice.

"Yameen is her husband."

"*Rukhsati* has not taken place as yet and he becomes her husband?" There was sarcasm in his voice.

"He became her husband, the moment their *nikah* was performed," Rehmatunnisa also managed to bring some authority in her voice.

"Now he will cease to be her husband. I will demand *talaq* for her. Yameen will have to send her a written *talaq*, Moulvi Sahib gave his final verdict. Saira was standing behind the blinds and listening to the unpleasant words of her father. He had hardly uttered the word *talaq*, when she ran out and fell at his feet. "*Abba Huzoor*, never utter that word again; give me your consent to join my husband," she begged.

"Do you know my child what Pakistan is?" Moulvi Sahib asked his daughter.

"No *Abba Huzoor*, I don't know," she said, "but I know that my husband is there. I wish to follow him wherever he goes."

"Pakistan is a rotten idea of the politicians who think that Muslims and Hindus should live separately. Pakistan is a place, my child, from where no one comes back. Pakistan is death," Moulvi Sahib said and burst into tears. It was a genuine outburst. It was a reaction of sheer helplessness. "You are my only child, if you go away who will I live for; what reason will there be for your mother to be alive?" Moulvi Sahib added in a voice choked with tears. The scene ended on a sad note. Even Rehmatunnisa went back, weeping, to her house.

But Moulvi Aijaz Ahmad's opinion about Pakistan, and his firm determination not to let his daughter go there, did not change. And the day arrived for Yameen's family to take the train for Lahore. Rehmatunnisa left her large house to her sister-in-law Ayesha, from whom, it was taken away by the custodian of Evacuee Property, in the course of a few months. Her larger zamindari, she left to the care of her Brahmin *ziledars* under the supervision of her brother-in-law Asghar, and sat down unwillingly in the train for Lahore with her five daughters. All her relatives including Moulvi Aijaz Ahmad, friends and neighbours, both Hindus and Muslims, stood on the railway platform to see her off. A little before the train gave its last whistle a young girl, clad in a black burqa, came like an arrow from one end of the platform and climbed into Rehmatunnisa's crowded compartment and almost fell into her lap. That was Saira. Even before anyone in the compartment could make out what had happened, Saira's father, who was like others standing on the platform, recognised her and barged into the compartment and tried unsuccessfully to pull her out. "No, my child you can't go. How can you leave your parents alone? You are not old enough to take such big decisions. Your marriage also is not complete. The *rukhsati* has yet to take place." Moulvi Aijaz Ahmad was laying down all the reasons he could to convince his daughter to change her mind. And Rehmatunnisa and her brother-in-law Asghar were persuading Moulvi Sahib to see reason. "Moulvi Sahib your daughter's marriage is legal and complete. She is twenty-one; she can take her own decisions. Above all, it is in her interest to join her husband and be with him." But Moulvi Sahib was adamant. Ultimately the police had to intervene. A Senior Inspector who was on duty on the platform, and who knew Asghar, said, "Vakeel Sahib, I also feel she should be allowed to go, but this is a sensitive moment. The father is not willing. When times are normal let her husband come, and take her away with him after a proper *rukhsati* ceremony."

A sobbing Saira was at last pulled out, by a policewoman, from the compartment. And the train whistled. Those present on the platform of Charbagh railway station on 16th December 1947 and those inside the train could not have erased from their memories the heart-rending wail of Saira as the train moved from the station towards a destination unknown to all those who sat in the train. And that wail was carried to Yameen's ears through his mother and sisters, the pain of which continued to ring in his ears ceaselessly through time.

When the postal system between the newly created country and India became effective, Yameen received one letter after another from Saira's father demanding a written *talaq* for Saira. In response Yameen sent just one letter in which he wrote that he had nothing against his wife Saira and so will never divorce her. Saira and Yameen, of course, wrote innumerable letters to each other but not one reached the other.

A year later another sincere effort was made by Yameen's family to unite the couple. Yameen's older uncle Akbar decided to leave for Pakistan. Both Akbar and his younger brother Asghar made several visits to Moulvi Aijaz Ahmad to request him for Saira's *rukhsati* to her husband's house.

"My young friends," Moulvi Sahib said, "her husband's home is now in Pakistan and not next door, in Hata-e-Kham Faqir Mohammad Khan. So I am no longer under any obligation to see that she joins him."

"What logic is that Moulvi Sahib," both the brothers asked.

"You will understand the logic when your daughters grow up and someone asks you to marry them to boys who live in a place from where there is no return ticket. If the groom or his parents had told us that they plan to settle in a country which their leaders are in the process of making, I would have broken Saira's engagement and not got the *nikah* performed."

There was disappointment once again. Akbar and his family had to leave without Saira.

Yet another effort failed two years later when Yameen's eldest uncle died in India and his family decided to leave for Pakistan. Yameen's relatives again requested Moulvi Aijaz Ahmad to send Saira with the family. And again Moulvi Sahib refused.

When all these efforts failed, Yameen requested the Pakistan government to give him permission to go to India to bring his wife. With great difficulty he got a "No Objection Certificate" from his department. He was also given a permit to travel to India. Till then there were no passports for travel between the two countries. But before he could leave for India, he got a long letter from Moulvi Sahib informing him of Saira's marriage to his wife's nephew. According to the letter the head maulana of a Muslim seminary had declared her earlier marriage null and void. Yameen's dreams had turned into nightmares long ago. Whatever hope he was left with, crashed after reading the letter. The name of Saira never crossed his lips again but he never consented to remarry. The topic of Lucknow, too, remained far from his conversations.

But Yameen did visit Lucknow again. Just once, forty years later, to see his favourite uncle, Asghar, who was eighty-seven and extremely ill with a liver problem. It was no easy decision for Yameen, but his uncle had been a source of great strength during his childhood and younger days. Asghar had also visited Pakistan twice when Yameen needed him most. It was time now for him to be near his uncle and his cousins. From Lucknow Airport Yameen, now sixty-four, drove with his cousins straight to Balrampur Hospital where his uncle was admitted.

"*Assalamalaikum Chachajan*," Yameen said to his uncle, and took both his hands to touch them to his wet eyes. To everyone's surprise, at least at that moment, Asghar looked as though he had never been ill.

"Forty years you stayed away from Lucknow, and when you came at last, it was to see me. Is that right?"

"Yes," Yameen agreed.

"I am really touched Yameen," Asghar said.

"*Chachajan* you have always stood by us in our difficult times. *Abba* and you have been my role models," Yameen replied.

Asghar felt embarrassed to hear all that praise from his nephew. He changed the direction of the conversation.

"I remember the day you were leaving Lucknow for joining the Central Secretariat Service at Delhi. You were in tears. I thought you would grab the first opportunity to dump the service and come back to Lucknow."

"I would have done exactly that, had I not got stuck in the web of that historical moment which had made India unrecognisable," Yameen said.

"Or if your father had lived. Usman *Bhaijan* would not have budged from Lucknow. He would have stayed back like me with his family. And even if option had been taken from you in favour of Pakistan, he would have called you back somehow." Asghar was talking as though it was 1947 and not 1987.

"You are absolutely correct. You know *Chachajan*, the borders were kept open till 1948 July, so that people could come back if they wanted. But I had called Amma and my sisters to Karachi imagining that the fire which was raging in Delhi, had reached Lucknow. What I saw in Delhi even from behind the security of the Purana Qila gave me the impression that India was not the place for Muslims. The scene was different in Lucknow, so I was told later. Had I been living in Lucknow the question of going to Pakistan would never have arisen." Yameen's eyes were getting wet again. For Asghar too, to fight that lump in his throat was not easy.

"Yameen, I think this amount of strain for *Mamujan* is enough for the day. It is time also for his doctors' rounds." Mahmud, who was Yameen's cousin and Asghar's sister's son, got up to take Yameen home for lunch and a little rest.

But Asghar asked for just another minute. "*Beta* Yameen, only last week we discovered that Saira is alive though she suffered from a long bout of tuberculosis. The family had shifted to Bhowali where she was in the sanatorium. After getting well she used her time to study further. Remember she had done her Metric, from that school near your house. Later she did MA LT. She never got married again. Her father wrote lies to you about her marriage. Here in Lucknow the rumour was, God forbid, that she had passed away. Allah be praised, she is fine. Both her parents are dead now. She retired last year as principal of a government college and lives here, in Lucknow."

For a moment Yameen lost his breath. For time endless, he stood like a statue, and then he said to his uncle as though in a dream, "*Chachajan*, where is she? I want to see her," Yameen could not control his restlessness. It was not happiness which had overpowered him. It was ecstasy.

"Go to her house, whenever you like, with Mahmud and your *chachi*. They know where she lives. We have not yet told her about your coming to Lucknow. Although I informed her, when I met her by chance in this very hospital last week, that Yameen never remarried," Asghar said gently.

"I want to go just know, Mahmud, let us not delay. Dulhan Chachi, you come with us," Yameen was impatient like a child.

A little later Yameen was standing outside a modest home in Thakurganj. A signboard on the door indicated that a lady whose name was Mrs Saira Yameen lived there. Yameen knocked and Saira opened the door. It took forty years for Yameen to reach her door and not even forty seconds for both of them to recognise each other. There was no falling into each others' arms; there were no exchange of words. The two of them stood there as though transfixed in time, in a strange dream. And then suddenly there was an endless flow of tears, from two pairs of eyes, which was determined to wash away the helplessness and deprivation of forty long years. Mahmud and Dulhan Chachi stood behind the wall for as long as they thought necessary and then came up, wiped their tears, found water for them to drink and made them sit down. And then, without a word, Saira got up, went into the next room and re-entered with a small suitcase. Yameen picked up the suitcase in one hand and held Saira's hand with the other. Dulhan Chachi said to Saira, "*Beta*, time has come for your *rukhsati* at last; it's time for you to leave this house and go to your real home which is where Yameen your husband lives."

And without a word, Saira and Yameen walked towards the waiting car.

A week or two later, when they were on their way to the Airport to take the flight for Pakistan, a cousin asked, "Who do you blame for delaying your *rukhsati* for forty long years and giving both of you a lifetime of excruciating pain?"

"No one," Saira and Yameen said together.

"Not even destiny?"

"No. destiny has its reasons!" Yameen said and Saira agreed.

Who did the Surgery on Her?

In the United Provinces of Agra and Awadh the British had set up the *taluqedars* as their most loyal supporters in the aftermath of the great uprising of 1857. They showered them with titles and land, but also saw to it that they did not blow their money on extravagant living alone, and instead used it for something worthwhile. The *taluqedars* were encouraged to give generous donations for building hospitals, schools and universities. Hospitals, there were in Lucknow, and so also universities, even during the rule of the nawabs, but when the British set up their first hospital in Lucknow, they called for donations from the landed gentry. An announcement was made that the hospital to be built would carry the name of the state which gave the largest donation. In that race, Balrampur left all *taluqedars* behind, and the great hospital built on a large stretch of green land cut off from the Residency, and fitted with the best medical facilities of the times, was called "Balrampur Hospital".

The place was full of neem and banyan trees. The buildings were not just surrounded by well-manicured lawns but interspersed with them. Hundreds of flower beds were spread on the lawns giving not only colour to the place but also cheer to the sick. The roads near and around the hospital were then, like most roads in Lucknow, peaceful; not crowded like the roads of today. The few people, who walked past, would stop by, just to let their eyes rest on the large stretches of green visible even from the road. Some would walk in for a little respite, if not stopped and questioned at the gate.

The place had some unpleasant structures too. These were graves mostly of those Englishmen who died during the 1857 revolt. They were screened, by hedges and bushes, from the common man's eyes with such subtlety, that except for those who worked in the gardens, no one noticed them, least of all, the patients.

Despite the beauty around and cleanliness and care within, Indians, during those times, did not think much of hospitals. Being admitted in a hospital meant that you had no one to care for you at home. The fear of dying in a hospital was so great that people avoided going there even for consulting specialists during emergencies. And yet, in Balrampur Hospital, both general and special wards were built for Indians, just as special wards were built exclusively for Europeans. This special wing had about ten big airy rooms each with an anteroom and a bathroom. All the rooms opened out into a wide veranda which faced a beautiful lawn. At the far end of the lawn was the back wall of the operation theatre which was hidden from the public view with rows of *amaltas* trees. Early summer would see them bursting into a lemon bloom. A yard or two away from the wall were the graves of two young British doctors who also perhaps lost their lives during the siege of the Residency. The *amaltas* trees also served to conceal them from public view.

The Emergency faced the main gate and was very close to it, as a hospital Emergency should be, for easy reach of patients. It was a cold December night in the year 1945. Christmas was round the corner. For the last six years, Lucknow, like other British ruled cities, had celebrated Christmas with severe austerity. But this year, it was going to be different. World War II, which had lasted for more than five years, was over and the citizens of Lucknow were determined to celebrate Christmas with a bang. While preparations for the big day were at their height, even at the dead of night in the city outside, a young English doctor sat shivering in the Emergency of the Balrampur Hospital. He was on duty. How he wished for a fireplace in his room and a couple of logs of wood. The neighbouring room, where the sister-in-charge and three staff nurses, sat huddled together, was as cold.

The quiet of the night was disturbed by the sound of a horse's hooves. A tonga stopped outside the Emergency. The doctor and the nurses heard the screams of the patient. They forgot about the severity of the weather and rushed out. Two ward boys reached the tonga with a stretcher. One of the staff nurses was ready with a warm blanket. In minutes the patient, a young Indian woman, along with her mother and husband, was inside the Emergency. The doctor examined the patient and diagnosed her with a severe problem of appendicitis. He recommended immediate surgery as, in his opinion, the appendix was about to burst. The husband was asked to give his consent, for surgery, in writing. As soon as he gave his consent, the nurses took the patient to prepare her for the operation and then wheeled her into the operation theatre.

In the meanwhile, the young doctor, on duty in the Emergency, took steps to call the surgeon. He sent a ward boy to his house, which was in the Hospital compound, with a file giving an account of his diagnosis of the patient's condition. Since the surgeon was the only doctor, apart from the senior superintendent, who was given a residential telephone by the government, he decided to call him on the phone. There was no direct dialling those days. Telephone lines were connected by operators sitting in the telephone exchange. Normally they were never absent from their seat, but that day, surprisingly, it was full ten minutes before the young doctor heard "Number please," from the operator. The more surprising part was that neither the surgeon nor anyone else at his residence answered the call. The ward boy, who had reached the house, without wasting any time, could also not communicate his message to the surgeon. The servants at his house took time to wake him up. He and his wife had gone to bed very late since their child was seriously ill. The result was that the surgeon reached the operation theatre almost an hour after the patient was put on the operating table.

As he stepped into the veranda outside the O.T., he saw the patient being wheeled out. For a moment he thought that the worst had happened. An hour's wait was too long for an appendix patient to survive. But then he saw glucose bottles attached to the patient. He walked nearer and could see the patient breathing. The surgeon recovered his confidence.

"Why are you bringing her out, take her in," he told the nurses present.

"What for?" the sister-in-charge asked.

The surgeon looked at the patient to check again if she was breathing. She was. The glucose too was moving in the tubes, and then he looked at the nurse and said sharply, "For the operation."

"How many times will she be operated upon?" the nurse asked.

The surgeon realised immediately that the surgery had been done, perhaps by the senior superintendent, who was an ace surgeon! His face fell. He was sure he would be penalised for dereliction of duty, perhaps suspended or dismissed from his government job. His delayed arrival for the surgery could have cost the patient her life. He became silent, but went with the patient to the Indian wing of the special ward, where she was being moved to, by the nurses. After the nurses had slipped her into the bed and fixed the glucose and medicine bottles correctly, they asked him to examine the patient, if he wanted.

He found the young lady doing fine. The operation was of course a success. Coming out of the ward he came face to face with the patient's mother and husband. Perhaps they wanted to know the condition. He told them that all was well and that the operation was a success. Both the relatives looked happy. The husband thanked him but said, to his dismay, "The Doctor Sahib who did the operation on my wife has already spoken to us!" The surgeon was once again reminded that his job was in danger.

The morning after, the errant surgeon expected to be called by the senior superintendent. When he was not called till noon, he mustered strength and went to the boss's room. He wanted to explain his position. "Come my boy," the senior superintendent said, as he entered the room, "I saw your patient during the morning rounds. You were not there. Obviously you were up most of the night. You've done a good job, and well in time. I think the girl will be back home in a day or two."

The Surgeon was dumbfounded. Was the boss resorting to sarcasm? And something terrible awaited him, something worse than what he feared!! He went back to the patient's room. She had regained her consciousness but was a wee bit drowsy. And, thank God, well on her way to recovery. He decided to wait for the evening to meet the young doctor in the Emergency and the nurses who had assisted in the O.T.

The young doctor assured him that he did not send for the senior superintendent. True, he couldn't reach him by phone but he was sure the ward boy would be able to get him. The surgeon was further confused. "May be the nurses called the senior superintendent, when I was delayed," he thought to himself and walked over to the nurses who were on duty in the O.T. the night before.

"But Doctor, why should we have called the senior superintendent?" asked one of the nurses.

"Because I was late," he said.

"You mean, to complain about you?"

"No, so that he could perform the surgery. He is the only other surgeon available in the hospital."

"But, Doctor, you were not at all late," the sister-in-charge said.

"I was. I came when you were wheeling out the patient back to the ward, after the operation," the surgeon said.

"Doctor, now stop joking and let us do our work," the sister-in-charge said. "If you came after the operation, then who did the operation?"

"You tell me, because you were present in the O.T.," the surgeon asked.

"I didn't," a cheeky young nurse, who was also on duty in the O.T., said and giggled.

"I didn't either," the other nurse, who was present there, said and laughed.

"Neither did I," said the sister-in-charge with a smile, "So off you go, Doc, and leave us to our work." The confusion in the surgeon's mind multiplied many fold. He decided to check on *his patient* before he went back home. The young woman was totally conscious and cheerful. She spoke to him in Urdu, "Doctor Sahib, I want to meet the doctor who performed the operation on me. I want to thank him."

"I did the operation," he said.

"You are joking Doctor Sahib," the woman said. "He was another doctor, also an *angrez* like you."

"How do you know? You were in extreme pain when you were taken to the O.T.," the surgeon asked.

"He spoke to me so affectionately and for a long time before he asked me to count backwards," she said. By then the surgeon was sure that the senior superintendent, who was also an Englishman, had performed the surgery on the woman. He became sure that she would recognise him when she saw him during the rounds, the following morning. "She will thank him to her heart's content and I will know my fate." The surgeon thought to himself.

The next morning when the senior superintendent went with his team on the rounds, the young lady showed no recognition. In fact she asked him to send the doctor who had done the surgery on her, so that she could thank him.

"Here he is, give him as much thanks as you want to," the senior superintendent pulled the surgeon by his hand, and made him stand right in front of her bed.

"No Doctor Sahib, he is not the one," she said vehemently, but no one took any notice of her and the team walked over to the next ward. For the surgeon, the mystery became deeper, too much of a burden for him to carry. Since the only other surgeon in the hospital was the senior superintendent, he decided to have a face to face conversation with him. He was not afraid of the consequences anymore. He confessed to him that he was not the one who had performed the surgery on the young lady. This time it was the boss who was in a state of shock. "And let me tell you, my dear friend, I am the only other surgeon in this hospital, and I swear, it was not me either, the Lord knows!"

When the nurses were questioned after being told that neither of the two hospital surgeons had operated upon the young lady, they had different answers to give. They admitted that it was their presumption that the resident surgeon had performed the operation!

"Sir," the senior nurse said, "during a surgery we concentrate on our ears and on the hands of the surgeon, so that we don't miss his orders and the hand given directions. Most of his face and hair, in any case, are covered."

But all three agreed on one point. That the surgeon in the O.T. was a European, with blue eyes and golden brown hair. The senior superintendent then asked, "From which side did you see him coming, through which door did he go out?" The nurses' memory was totally blank on these points. But all agreed that when they saw the resident surgeon in the veranda outside the O.T., after the operation, they thought that he had came out from the O.T. with them after doing the surgery!

The mystery became deeper and deeper. It was decided to end the matter there. All four, the three nurses and the resident surgeon came out of the senior superintendent's room after taking an oath that they will not talk about the incident or about their doubts ever. They apparently did keep the sanctity of the oath till the young patient was discharged. Obviously not, thereafter.

After the young lady was discharged, she went with her husband and mother to meet the nurses who were in the O.T. during her operation. Each one of them carried a beautiful rose garland. The girl said, "We brought these garlands for the doctor sahib who performed the operation and gave me life, but the big Doctor Sahib has told us that he has gone on long leave. After him, we think it is you three who deserve these garlands." The nurses took the garlands, with thanks, to avoid any discussion.

They put one garland on the cornice just under the large painting of the Sacred Heart of Jesus, "What should we do with the other two garlands?" one staff nurse enquired.

"We will place them where they most deserve to be placed," the sister-in-charge said.

The following morning, when the gardener was cleaning the space behind the *amaltas* trees, he saw a faded rose garland on each of the two graves of the young European doctors which were just a yard or two away from the back wall of the Balrampur Hospital operation theatre.

*The Rat**

It was past five in the evening, Prabhakar was about to leave office, when the deputy office superintendent rushed into his room. He carried a cyclostyled letter in his hand and a grin on his face.

"Sir, good news for you. Your transfer orders to Delhi." He handed over the orders to Prabhakar, and continued, "The order was in the dak pad which I sent for your kind perusal. Perhaps your 'good self' missed it."

Prabhakar's 'good self' would have missed even a love letter, if it was mixed up in the office dak pad. He was not one of those who would waste much time or attention over a 'routine matter' as office dak! He took the letter from the official, expressed his thanks with a condescending smile, and left for home, through the door opened for him by two uniformed peons. Anyone would have welcomed the idea of leaving Ladakh. Prabhakar too, was overjoyed to get a posting nearer home. But he remembered to keep an expressionless face. He did not believe in expressing any emotion before his subordinates. It spoilt the discipline of the office.

---

* This story first appeared in *Sunday Statesman* on 20 November 1977.

But he wrote about the transfer to his parents, immediately, and also told them to fix up the earliest possible date for his marriage. He and his parents had at last accepted a match for him. During the last eight years, since he had joined service, he had been examining proposals and rejecting them on some ground. Marriage, Prabhakar felt, was not something one should plunge into, in haste, on emotional or sentimental considerations. One should weigh the pros and cons of the match from all angles and then take a decision. One never loses by waiting. In fact the chances of getting a younger bride become brighter. Prabhakar was conscious of the fact that he was a member of the superior-most civil service of the country. He had a long way to go. And anyone, wanting to hand-over charge of his daughter to him, should deserve to be his father-in-law.

At last Prabhakar's parents had found such a deserving man, who had, first of all, influence to push Prabhakar up the ladder of bureaucracy. And secondly, who had pots and pots of money to give him the luxurious life which a member of the Heaven-born service deserves. This deserving man had happened to have sired a daughter who was submissive, well versed in domestic chores and who had no personal ambitions. So after all Prabhakar was right. In the marriage market a man does not lose by waiting, like a woman does.

When Prabhakar took over his new charge in the ministry in Delhi, he was so full of his prospective marriage and his father-in-law-to-be, that he did not even miss the pomp of the district charge he had just left. He was too dazzled by his own future to brood over his newly acquired anonymity—a painful experience for most officers who have to sit in pigeon holes of the Central Secretariat after having held the sceptre in a small district. Before long Prabhakar's colleagues in the ministry had known all there was to know about his influential and wealthy in-laws-to-be. And one must admit, there were few who were not impressed with Prabhakar's luck.

One day when everyone was assembled in one of the rooms for lunch, Ganguli, one of Prabhakar's colleagues, walked in with his batchmate Meher Rangoonwala. She needed no introduction. Some knew her personally, others had heard about this girl from Lucknow. For once Prabhakar forgot about the influence and contacts his prospective marriage was to bring him. He had briefly met this girl at Ladakh when she had gone there on a trek with some friends. Prabhakar remembered how two of the girls had taken seriously ill. Meher had asked for his help to have them flown back. Today when he saw this well proportioned woman draped in a red bordered yellow saree, she struck him as positively beautiful. In Ladakh he had dismissed her as a stupidly reckless woman. He had always held that women were ridiculously ill suited for sports like mountaineering and trekking. Meher stayed in the room for a short time, exchanged a few words with those who spoke to her and then left; and with her left the glow from the faces of all those present. But her brief visit set all of them talking. Srinivasan showed his surprise about her not joining them for lunch. "Earlier she'd never refuse a meal with us," he said.

"In search of pastures new, old chap," Bannerji gave the only reason which came to his mind and looked around for applause, which he got in abundance.

"You are right," Gupta agreed. "We've all been tried, one by one, but found wanting." A sky piercing laughter followed.

"You'll bring down the building *yaar*," Ganguli chided them for their lack of restraint. "Perhaps she has too much work on her desk these days."

"Work my foot; this is the first time I've heard of a lady officer having to work." Srinivasan's remarks evoked the earlier response again.

"But Miss Rangoonwala has a reputation for efficiency. She has proved to be quite a success in the district also," Ganguli reminded them, gently.

"Ganguli, *yaar*, you have no brains. With her sexy figure, and her *Lucknavi ada* anyone would have been a success." Gupta made in the air with his two index fingers, what, he thought, should be the figure of a sexy woman.

"She has earned good reports for herself with her intelligence and her work." It was surprising how Ganguli was braving the situation.

"Put in my chuckle, oh God, that silvery tinkle and I'll get from my bosses what Miss Rangoonwala has got from hers." Gupta made a fake prayer to the almighty and brought the house down.

To this debate, Prabhakar could contribute nothing. He only joined his colleagues in their laughter. But Miss Rangoonwala's visit had done something peculiar to Prabhakar. He could think of nothing else but her. Back in his own room, he started thinking of ways and means of getting to know her better. That very afternoon he decided to visit her in her office which was on the first floor in the same building. Prabhakar had initial nervousness but then he argued himself into a confident attitude. The conversation of his colleagues had convinced Prabhakar that Meher was easily available, not that he didn't have his own personal opinion of working women. A woman nearing thirty, according to Prabhakar, would grab any male company which came her way. He was lucky that he was still a bachelor. Meher may develop hopes of a marriage with him, that is what all women want ultimately, no matter what status or society they belong to. His chances were indeed bright. That is what Prabhakar thought as he entered Miss Rangoonwala's room.

Meher was bent over a file and two officers stood near her. As she raised her head to discuss the case with her officers, she saw Prabhakar, and gave him an absent smile. Motioning him, with her hand, to sit down, she continued to discuss the case. That took full twenty minutes, in the meanwhile other files kept piling up. Prabhakar felt uneasy and humiliated. That was not the way a colleague should be treated. But he did not want to give up. He decided to pacify himself. Perhaps this was a technique which women used to impress their menfolk and keep them around. At last Meher put her thoughts on the note sheet and signed. She looked up and smiled at Prabhakar, apologised for having kept him waiting, rang the bell, and ordered tea for two. And Prabhakar forgot about the humiliation he felt a little while ago.

"I wonder if you remember having met me before." Prabhakar wanted to say something.

"How can I ever forget that?" Meher was thinking of the help he had rendered in evacuating some members of her trekking team who had taken seriously ill in Ladakh. Her words helped to calm Prabhakar's nerves. His posture, on the chair he was sitting on, became more relaxed. He asked her where she stayed, and spoke of his own housing problem.

"It is not difficult to get the type of flat I'm staying in. I think if you apply now, you'll get it within a month. The location is central, but it is too small for a family." Meher was right. Hers was a two-roomed apartment which could not accommodate a family. One really doesn't know how far Prabhakar was right in interpreting Meher's words as a smooth way of finding out his marital status. But such an interpretation suited Prabhakar, and he decided to cash in on his last days of bachelorhood.

"You see, I am a bachelor, I do not need much space, but I think I should see the flat before I apply to the director of Estates," he paused, took a few puffs at his cigarette and then resumed with a jerk, as though an idea had suddenly occurred to him.

"If it is not very inconvenient for you, I could drop in at your flat and see for myself how the accommodation would suit me."

"By all means," Meher's acceptance was nothing more than her *Lucknavi* courtesy. But Prabhakar took unusual care to dress before he reached her flat at the appointed time.

Prabhakar saw the apartment. When Meher went into the kitchen to get him some coffee, he felt that, that would be too much trouble for her.

"Why don't we have coffee at Ramble's? As it is, I have put you to so much trouble."

Meher was embarrassed and irritated as well, though with her breeding and innate decency she masked her true feelings. The least she could do was to give her guest a cup of coffee.

A visit to Ramble's was not at all called for. She did not care for such social outings, which according to her were at the root of all office gossip, however innocuous they might be.

"It is no trouble at all to make a cup of coffee. I am quite at home in the kitchen." Meher said this just to put him at ease. But Prabhakar chose to read more into the simple statement. He was determined, in any case, to feel at home. His visit left no mark on Miss Rangoonwala's mind, or on her heart. But that visit became the most hotly discussed issue among Prabhakar's office colleagues and among his friends.

"So the dame first extracted from you information about your marital status, and then volunteered information about her adeptness in the kitchen," Srinivasan was telling Prabhakar.

"Hinting thereby that you will not regret marrying a girl who is good in household affairs." Bannerji added his bit.

"I knew from the start, that the moment she discovers that our Prabhakar is unmarried, she'll leave no stone unturned to get him," was Gupta's claim.

"But surely she knows our hero is to tie the knot soon and gain an influential father-in-law in the bargain? I feel she was being decent, a good hostess, a good colleague," Ganguli, silent so far, could not help adding.

"How could she know or be sure? Hey Ganguli, you are forgetting *yaar*. Remember when invitations went on pouring at Khalid Imamuddin. He had no alternative but to visit her. One should hear from the poor chap how he had to almost run out of her house to save his dear life."

"And chastity," Gupta completed, amidst laughter, the incident which Srinivasan was reminding them about.

These exchanges with his colleagues further strengthened Prabhakar's hopes. He was convinced that good luck was in store for him. His heart wanted to have a fling. His head told him to wait and see, and make sure that such a thing does not place any obstacles in the way of his marriage. After deliberation with self, Prabhakar got the green signal.

Ever since his marriage was fixed in that influential and rich family, Prabhakar had always found time to thank the Almighty for bestowing such good luck on him. He knew that after his marriage his life would be one long smooth road to happiness and success. The least he could do was to give some moments, though brief, of happiness to others also. It was with these generous thoughts that Prabhakar went up the lift of the multi-storeyed building that housed the 'lonely soul' which he wished to 'redeem.'

At ten minutes to eleven, when the evening sounds and bustle had almost died down, Prabhakar was pressing the bell outside Miss Meher Rangoonwala's house. A dim ray of light from one room and the sound of music told Prabhakar that Meher was awake. A sleepy eyed ayah appeared at the doorstep and informed that the mistress had retired for the night. Prabhakar insisted that his work was urgent, and went past the ayah into the dimly lit room. Meher was at the piano. Since her schooldays in Lucknow, her involvement with music had not diminished, in spite of a full-time job. In fact she was practising for a recital which she had to give around the weekend. Meher was surprised and angry at the untimely intrusion.

"Is there some emergency?" She questioned Prabhakar, curtly, her face stern with none of its usual softness.

"I did not know you played the piano so well. It is a novel experience indeed to see the hand, which wields the pen so effectively, striking such melodious notes." Prabhakar ignored Meher's question, thinking flattery would get him what he wanted, without effort.

"I asked you a question," Meher's eyes were burning and her voice was cold.

Prabhakar brought all the pathos he could in his voice, "Now Meher, does there have to be an emergency for me to come to you? Don't pretend that you don't know what my heart is going through from the day I set eyes on you."

Meher was taken aback. Before she could react Prabhakar grabbed her hands and said, "There is no need for these fingers to move aimlessly on the piano keyboard, let them rest in the warmth of my hands."

This was more than Meher could have imagined. Normally she avoided making a scene before servants. On this occasion she found no alternative but to roughly pull her hand away from his and push him against the wall. She then proceeded to call the ayah.

Prabhakar was dumbfounded. All his plans had misfired. However, his convictions led him on to make a last ditch effort. "Please don't misunderstand my intentions, I want to marry you. I want you as my legally wedded wife, only you can give me happiness." He thought that this surely was his trump card.

"Marry you indeed! And who ever told you that I was waiting till now to marry a rat like you? Get out, you disgraceful rat, and don't ever sneak into people's houses at the dead of night with the hope of nibbling at anything lying unprotected. Get out before I call the guard and make your disgrace public."

The next moment Prabhakar was coming out of Miss Rangoonwala's flat. He indeed felt like a rat, a rat cruelly trapped, but an unusual trap this was, it was laid by the Rat himself.

The following day Miss Rangoonwala made it a point to be present at the lunch club which Prabhakar attended. She had earlier warned her batchmate Ganguli that she was coming and had requested him to ensure that everyone was there. The moment Prabhakar saw her, he mumbled something and headed for the door.

"Mr Prabhakar, please don't leave. A friend of mine arrived from Lucknow this morning and brought some kababs. I want to share them with all of you." Meher was determined not to let Prabhakar run away.

"I am a vegetarian," Prabhakar was too nervous to find a proper excuse for leaving the room.

"So what! There are many here who are vegetarians. They are not leaving." Ganguli said and pulled Prabhakar by the hand and forced him into a chair.

"Are these *tunday kababs*?" Bannerji asked.

"They are made by someone who has both his hands intact," Meher said.

"What do you mean–both hands?" Bannerji was perplexed.

"The first man who made these kababs and sold them at Akbari Gate, had only one hand, the other one was amputated. *Tunday* is an Urdu/Hindi word for someone who has only one hand!" Meher explained.

"Interesting story!" Gupta said.

"No, interesting fact," Meher corrected, "and I have a more interesting and more recent fact to share with all of you."

"Go ahead Miss Rangoonwala, we are all ears," Gupta said, and everyone pulled their chairs towards the table and looked a personification of attention. Only Prabhakar wriggled in his chair. He looked as though he was about to hear the pronouncement of a death sentence.

"First ask Mr Prabhakar whose house he had gatecrashed into at 11 pm last night and for what purpose," Meher asked her eager audience.

All eyes turned towards Prabhakar. And there was not a single person there who didn't address him with a question.

"Where did you go?"

"*Kahan gaye the*?"

"We want an answer."

"Fast."

"*Jaldi*."

And Prabhakar looked a picture of shame.

And then Meher began her narration of all that happened at her flat the previous night. She left no detail, including Prabhakar's proposal of marriage to her, and how she called him "a rat" and said "do you think I was waiting so long to marry a rat like you?" And how she finally pushed him out of the house. Prabhakar said nothing, but made a last effort to leave. Ganguli pushed him back into the chair. "Wait a minute. Let the lady leave first. It is bad manners to precede a lady." As Meher closed her lunchbox, put it in her bag, and was about to leave she turned around again. She looked at every one present and said, "Even women have their choices and priorities. And this is for all of you. I advise you to get rid of your imaginary notions about your women colleagues. The sooner you do it the better for you."

And this time it was not just Prabhakar, but many others who turned pale and were wriggling in their chairs.

When a Jagir Went Abegging

"It was the best of times; it was the worst of times." This was what Dickens said of the times in France during the Revolution. I could say the same of the times when the Mutiny spread over north India and turned it upside down. Readers will have no problem believing that it was the worst of times and demand no explanation. But I definitely will have to explain, why those times were the best of times.

In my opinion, those were the best of times also because, at last, the Indian had plucked up courage to stand up against the unfair rule of the British. This was no Sepoy Mutiny as the British wanted us to believe, but an uprising of the people, and a bold one at that. It was another matter that success dodged the Indian at that time, but the fire within him continued to burn till he forced the British to leave the Indian shores in 1947. I have other reasons also to call those times the best of times. There were happenings during the Mutiny which showed the Indian in a happy light, as the incident which centred round Meer Syed Hussain, who lived in a *mohalla* called Barood Khana in Lucknow.

His was a house which was not very big, just enough to be comfortable for his mother, his wife, his three minor children and a nephew. There were two entrances to his house, one through the *deorhi*, by the side of the *baithak*. The other entrance, which was only used by the sweeper, was through the toilet. The sweeper entered through this door and left by the same one after cleaning the toilet. A narrow covered gully called *kulia* connected his house to that of his mother-in-law, who was also his aunt, his mother's sister. In the courtyard of her house there was a window which opened into Nana Abba's house. Nana Abba was Meer Sahib's grandfather. Now Nana Abba's house had a door through which one could walk into Jumman's house, which was on the main road in another locality called Golaganj. Jumman was Nana Abba's faithful servant to whom he had given the house. Servants were mainly lodged on the main roads, whereas masters lived in the interior part of the *mohallas* for the sake of security and safety.

There were about half a dozen other houses which led into each other, through terraces and *mokhas*. All the houses could be reached without taking recourse to the road. So if an Indian who was being chased by a *firangi*, got into Jumman's house in Golaganj, he could reach Barood Khana or Mumtaz Mahal ka Hata through the interconnecting windows, *kulias* and *mokhas*, and disappear without leaving any traces for the foreigner to pursue him. During the Mutiny the British were paranoid of this type of interconnectivity and also of streets which ended in cul-de-sacs. The first thing they did after putting down the insurrection was to demolish these houses and build roads through them.

Meer Syed Hussain was sleeping, as was his family, in the house the main door of which was in Barood Khana, when there was a loud knock on his door, a little after midnight in June 1857. The siege of the Residency had yet not begun, but the city had become a battlefield. The 48th native infantry had risen against their British bosses. The Regiments had mutinied and so also the Police. Lucknow was definitely not the place where anyone should have responded to a knock at midnight. But Meer Syed Hussain promptly got up, lit a lantern, and proceeded towards the main door through the *deorhi*. His mother ran after him.

"Where are you going; what are you up to?" his mother whispered.

"Amma don't worry. Only someone who needs me urgently would come to my door at this hour," Meer Sahib whispered back.

"There are children in this house and there is your young wife. Supposing the enemy rushes in?" His mother kept her voice low.

"Then you and Begum can pick up the children and run to Khala Amma's house. What is the *kulia* for? And if need be to Nana Abba's house and in case of further danger into Jumman's house."

"Don't make a joke of it, *Beta*. The times are dangerous," his mother warned.

"Amma, an enemy does not knock before entering. The one who is knocking, is in desperate need of help, I am sure. He has come to this door with confidence that the door will be opened to him." And Meer Sahib proceeded towards the door. As he unlatched it, he saw before him a man whom he recognised. He was Laddan, the cook of an Englishman.

"What brings you here at this time of the night?" Meer Sahib asked Laddan.

"*Huzoor*," the cook said, "my master's seven-year-old daughter is missing since early morning. We have looked for her everywhere. Since you are so helpful, and the city is so well known to you, I decided to ask you for your help."

"But Laddan Mian, this is no time to go on a child searching mission. It is pitch dark. There are no streetlights. The roads must be infested with mutineers," Meer Sahib said.

"Sir, in such times if we wait till the morning it may be too late. The parents are devastated." Laddan himself was in tears. Meer Sahib was touched by the concern which Laddan showed for his master's daughter. He could imagine what the condition of the parents would be. Meer Sahib said nothing more. He went in, changed his clothes, asked his mother to bolt the door, lifted the lantern and accompanied Laddan.

They went together through the streets of Lucknow over dead bodies and debris of bombed buildings. There was no luck till the wee hours of the morning. The June heat was making things more difficult for them. When the day dawned, they found themselves very close to the Baillie Guard. As they walked under the banyan tree, which was close to the place, they heard someone sobbing. They stopped to check and felt some movement in the branches of the tree. The sobbing stopped. They were about to move ahead, when they heard a soft voice call out, "Khansama, Khansama."

They knew that someone was on the tree and calling out to Laddan Mian.

Meer Sahib climbed up on to the lowest branch and could see a European child perched up on the tree. He called Laddan to come up so that the child could see him and regain her confidence. Both of them helped the child to come down the tree. She was indeed the child they were looking for. They went straight to the Englishman's house and delivered the girl to her parents. All three were mad with joy. "I see in you our saviour," the Englishman told Meer Sahib.

"You are not a human being, you are an angel," the child's mother said. The Englishman embraced his *bawarchi* and Meer Sahib, and kissed them on their forehead. Meer Sahib said, "Don't give us any credit sir; it was the will of God that we could find your child. Let us thank the Almighty."

Meer Sahib did not wait, not even to have a glass of water. He left immediately. He wanted nothing to interfere with the reunion of the child with her parents. And above all he was also desperate to reach home. He knew that no one in his family could have had a moment of peace after he left the house at that unearthly hour. "They must be expecting the worst," he thought to himself. And he was right.

When he reached his house he found the entire *mohalla* gathered there to give support to his family. Immediately on his return, thanksgiving prayers were offered by his mother and wife and sweets were distributed among all present, which included both Hindus and Muslims.

Time moved on. And the tables were turned. The Lucknow Residency was relieved in November 1857. The insurrection was put down by the British all over India. The rule of East India Company came to an end, and India became part of the great empire under the British Crown.

And then one day, when Meer Syed Hussain had all but forgotten the midnight knock and his walking through gunshots and bombings with Laddan Bawarchi to look for that lost little English child, he was called to the deputy commissioner's office! He had no idea what lay in store for him, till he was told that a *jagir* was being offered to him as reward for his loyalty to the British.

"*Huzoor,*" Meer Sahib addressed the deputy commissioner, "your humble servant is not aware how and where his loyalty to the British government was taken note of."

"Meer Sahib," the deputy commissioner said, "you helped an Englishman to find his dear daughter at a risk to your own life."

"Sir," Meer Sahib said, "I did not go at midnight to look for the child due to any loyalty to the British government. It was to help the *bawarchi* who came to me, in tears, asking for my help. My heart went out to the devastated parents, who happened to be British. I did nothing out of the way, nor anything extraordinary. It was just good luck and God's will that we found the child. Kindly forgive me, but I will not accept the *jagir*, or any other award. If anyone deserves the award it is indeed Laddan Bawarchi, the faithful servant of the English couple."

And Meer Sahib came back home empty handed. Before returning, he exaggerated and elaborated, before the British officials, the role of Laddan in finding the child.

Some months later, it was Laddan Bawarchi who was offered a *jagir* for loyalty to the British government. He also refused, on the same grounds as Meer Sahib, and further added, "My award was reuniting the child to her parents."

Why did Asif-ud-Daulah Build the Great Imambara?

One never heard of the title of Prince being given either by the nawabs or by the British to the nobility of Awadh nor to the descendants of the kings of Awadh. Yet Haris Hussain's signboard had the prefix of Prince before his name. The army of servants he had in his haveli addressed him as *Shehzade Huzoor* and his wife as *Shehzadi Begum*. His two sons were *Bare Shehzade* and *Chote Shehzade*, and his daughter who was born fifteen years after the younger son was called *Shehzadi Bitiya*. Outsiders and friends referred to him, most respectfully as 'Prince'.

He could have been a descendant of the son of the Mughal Emperor Shah Alam II who was settled in Lucknow and whose children had married in the family of the rulers of Awadh. But one is not sure. Prince Haris Hussain lived in a huge haveli in Aminabad, more towards the Moulvi Ganj side. It spread out in an acre or two of land. It was surrounded by gardens and lawns like the British bungalows.

Unlike other aristocrats of the times, he was given British education, apart from Arabic, Persian and Urdu. He did his schooling from La Martinere and studied law at the newly established University of Lucknow which had received a large donation from his father. But that law degree was never used by him in any way. He sent his two sons to Sherewood in Nainital and had plans for sending them to England for higher studies. But both dropped out from school and fell into bad ways.

He showed a lot of interest in the education of his daughter too, whom he sent to the only convent that Lucknow had in the 1940s. She did very well throughout school. But when she reached Senior Cambridge, much to everyone's surprise, she was withdrawn from school. The reason being that the Senior Cambridge examination was held, for all girls and boys of Lucknow schools, in one large hall of La Martinere Boys' School. The objection was raised not by Prince Haris Hussain but by his two worthless sons.

"*Abba Huzoor*, educating your daughter at the convent was alright. Everyone knew that Zehra went to school under strict purdah and sat with girls in class and played only with them. There were no boys in the school after second standard. Only Irish nuns and lady teachers taught her. But for the Senior Cambridge examination she will be sitting with boys." The younger brother gave his reasons for not letting his sister continue with her studies.

"I will ensure that she gets a desk right at the back of the hall, with all girls around her and the boys right in front." Prince Haris Hussain was confident that he would be able to convince the authorities.

"Don't forget *Abba Huzoor* that there will be male invigilators who will walk up and down the hall to ensure discipline among the examinees," the older brother turned down his father's reasoning.

"Everyone knows that Senior Cambridge examinations are conducted with no consideration for *purdah-nashin* girls. It will be a shame to your much respected name, *Abba Huzoor*," the younger boy chipped in again.

For days the debate continued but the person, whose life and future was at stake, was not given space or time to express her opinion. Zehra just watched and waited for the best. Her parents did fight out her case with great zeal but finally gave up. Why did her father turn weak before his worthless sons, why did he let their opinion prevail, was not easy for Zehra to understand. She was heartbroken. She had done so well in school and hoped to get a first division in Senior Cambridge. The nuns and teachers were also very sad. It was difficult for them too to understand why the father couldn't put his foot down and tell his worthless sons to mind their own business. After all, he was the head of the family, the owner of all the wealth.

Life for Zehra after that was years and years of depression. Marriage did not come her way either, because her parents could not find a suitable match for her. In the early 1950s most good families and educated boys had crossed over to Pakistan. Prince Haris Hussain's wealth had also started dwindling, particularly after the abolition of the zamindari system. The wealth he had inherited could have been enough for him and his family to lead a life of plenty. But for his lifestyle and for the lifestyle of his alcoholic sons no amount of money was enough. There were no other sources of income except for the wealth and houses he had inherited. He did nothing to reduce the retainers and hangers-on in his *deorhi*. He had no bad habits himself but his sons and their wives made up for that. His own fondness for throwing parties and organising music and dance soirees with regular frequency dug into his wealth with an unimaginable speed.

By the middle of the 1950s he had sold four other houses which he had, but did not allow his lifestyle to suffer a change. He continued to entertain worthless people at *mujras* and music parties. The retainers and hangers-on continued to throng his *deorhi* and his two sons continued to dig holes in his purse. His attention was focussed only on ensuring that no one got to know that his financial assets had reduced in any way.

Soon there came a time when there were no more houses and lands left to be sold, except the haveli in which he lived and entertained his friends. The haveli was enormous. Maintaining it was not easy. But selling a part of it would have exposed his financial condition. After much thought, he decided to sell the jewellery and the priceless decoration pieces, the chandeliers and paintings. But selling all that also had to be kept under wraps. His eyes fell on a beautiful jade flower vase. But he could not make out how to go about selling it, or for that matter, any other item. He did not know anybody who would buy it. And above all the sale had to be conducted in absolute secrecy. If anyone got to know his *izzat* would be destroyed. He decided to take his wife into confidence.

"Shehzadi Begum, how do we go about our lives now? All the money has been spent. There's nothing left now even to sell, except, please forgive me, your jewellery and other household things."

"My jewellery and all these decoration pieces are all yours, use them as you like, but even all this will not last you forever," Shehzadi Begum replied.

"You are right, what can we do then," the prince said in a tone of extreme helplessness.

"Stop entertaining your friends with *mujras* and music parties. Throw out your hangers-on, reduce the servants. This is the only solution," the wife said firmly.

"I appreciate what you say, but we cannot stop these things suddenly. If done gradually the people will not notice it," the prince suggested with all the gentleness he could muster.

"Don't be under the illusion that people haven't noticed what you think you have swept under the carpet. They have. It is time you thought about the marriage of your daughter. All the priceless items you are thinking of selling to keep up appearances before society, should be sold to get money to be spent on her wedding," the princess had her priorities in place, but no one ever asked her for her advice.

"Who would be more concerned about Zehra's marriage than me but first of all a suitable proposal should come for her," the prince said.

"You have to try for a suitable proposal," the wife answered.

"What do you mean Shehzadi Begum, a girl's father should go around asking people to marry his daughter? This has never happened in our society. *Paighams* come from the boy's side," the prince appeared quite hurt.

"*Paighams* have come, but you have not found a single one up to your level," Shehzadi Begum complained.

"Obviously I will not marry our daughter below our status," the prince replied, and in the same breath continued to say, "but Shehzadi Begum the priority just now is how do we run the kitchen." Both of them knew that the money left with them would just about manage a meal. For tomorrow there was nothing. He told her about the jade flower vase which stood on a stool in a corner in the ladies' sitting room. It was a very expensive piece and could keep the kitchen fire burning for at least a week, provided they found a buyer who appreciated its value. No one was likely to notice its absence. But where does one find such a buyer who would not disclose where he bought it from.

"I think we will have to consult Baqar Mian. Call him and take his advice," the wife suggested. Baqar Mian was their housekeeper. His main job was to supervise the kitchen. He was responsible for the entertainment and looking after of guests and visitors. Baqar Mian in fact kept an eye on the entire haveli, the servants, retainers and hangers-on.

The prince called Baqar Mian thrice and sent him back with some irrelevant instructions. He could not gather courage to tell him that he wished to sell the jade flower vase because there was no money left in the house. At last it was decided that the princess should call him and consult him about the sale.

"Shehzadi Begum it would be easier for you to talk to him about this embarrassing problem, because you won't be face to face with him. You will be talking to him from behind the curtain."

"You are right I will call him in a minute and talk to him, but as soon as I come to the point you should walk in," she said to her husband.

"I will do that, don't worry," the prince said and went to the adjoining room and stood at the door waiting for his cue to walk in.

Soon Baqar Mian knocked at the door, stood at a distance from the curtain and said, "*Adab baja lata hoon* Shehzadi Huzoor. What orders do you have for your humble servant?"

"I have to take your advice on a very minor issue," the princess said, softly.

"Shehzadi Huzoor, *ghulam* is all attention," she replied.

"There is a jade flower vase which is lying in an insignificant corner of the ladies' sitting room. It fulfils no purpose and is quite useless for us. We can easily dispense with it," the princess began.

"*Baja farmaya Huzoor nay,*" Baqar Mian said.

"But it is a priceless piece nevertheless," the princess said and added, "Will it be possible for you to find a buyer for it?"

Baqar Mian was suddenly taken aback. He didn't expect the princess to put before him a proposal for sale of an object belonging to the haveli. Thank God the princess could not see the shock on his face from behind the curtain. She would never have been able to continue with the proposal. But the prince darted out from the next room when his wife uttered the word 'buyer'. And then he casually strolled towards the door where his wife stood.

"What! Shehzadi Begum you are giving instructions to Baqar Mian for tonight's dinner?" he said to his wife loud enough for Baqar Mian's ears.

"No no! It is still too early for dinner. Remember the jade vase I told you about," the princess said to her husband.

"Yes yes you said something about it being of no use. Shehzadi Begum why don't you give it to someone if you don't like it," he said very casually.

"But it is a rare and priceless piece. I was asking Baqar Mian to find a buyer for it; we could then buy something in its place. Something of today's taste."

"Good idea. What does Baqar Mian have to say? Can he find a buyer?" The prince tried to sound indifferent, and casually crossed from between the curtains into the veranda where Baqar Mian was standing.

"I will try my best to abide by your orders," he said, "Though I have really never sold anything before. You know that *Huzoor*." The prince pretended to move in the direction of his room but suddenly turned back giving the impression intentionally, that an idea had struck him.

"Baqar Mian, it would be better if you tell the buyer that the vase is yours, otherwise it would be a shame for this haveli."

"*Huzoor* if I say it is mine the vase will be considered ordinary and cheap. It will fetch a good price only if I say that it is from this haveli," Baqar Mian explained.

"Then you could tell the buyer that my father gave it to you on your wedding. Or somehow get a word from him that he will not tell anyone else that the vase was sold by us," the prince requested Baqar Mian and added very graciously, "You see, Shehzadi Begum is adamant to sell it, and I have never denied her anything."

"I will try my best *Huzoor*. The *izzat* of this haveli is of supreme importance to me," Baqar Mian said. He took the jade flower vase, put it in a bag and left for Raja Bazar. He knew that only the Rastogis would buy such a priceless and rare item. Baqar Mian had already been approached by some of them. After the prince had sold his four houses, word had travelled around that his financial condition was not what it used to be. People in Raja Bazar knew about the precious items which decorated the haveli. The price which the Rastogis gave for the jade flower vase was so good that it surprised not only Baqar Mian but also the prince and his wife.

It was with the help of such drama that the selling spree began in the haveli of Prince Haris Hussain. But it was not long, before all rare and priceless items and jewellery had moved out from the prince's haveli and reached Raja Bazar. The heavy price which the prince received for the jade flower vase was never repeated, though more expensive things were sold. Throughout the selling spree the prince's only concern was that the buyer kept it a secret. He did not want people to know that he was reduced to penury. The two sons of the prince also lent a helping hand in speeding up the clearance. Soon the haveli was shorn of all its adornments. But life survived and had to be fed and clothed. The only thing left to be sold was the haveli. The prince first sold half of it and then gradually the rest of it. Three rooms which were earlier occupied by servants remained for the owners. The place where the imposing haveli stood looked like a slum now. People lived on all sides. It was difficult to find a way to approach those rooms where the prince lived with his family. With the feasting and partying gone, the hangers-on also disappeared. The servants had to find new jobs for themselves as well. Only Baqar Mian was left under a thatched roof which he had put over a tiny part of the lawn, near the well, which remained with the family. Baqar Mian had saved enough from his salary and from the cuts and commissions. His son had got the job of a peon with the Shiah Waqf Board and he lived separately. All said and done he was the only faithful servant of the prince who refused to leave his master. As a matter of fact it was he who saw to it that his master and mistress and their daughter did not starve. The prince's two sons had earlier moved with their wives to their in-laws' homes.

One August morning after a shower of rain the prince was sitting near the well, in that strip of the lawn which remained with him, to enjoy a little cool breeze. Suddenly he saw a suited-booted man approaching him. With him were the prince's two sons.

Looking at their father the two sons bent double for an "*adab*" and then the elder son said, "*Abba Huzoor*, this gentlemen was eager to meet you, he asked me to introduce him to you."

"What is his name, who is he?" The father asked with doubt spread all over his face.

"I do not know his name *Abba Huzoor*, but he told me that he owned some hotels in Lucknow and in other places in India," the son replied.

"You did not even care to find out his name and you dared to bring him into my presence to introduce him to me." Then turning to the man he said, "I do not talk to people whose complete introduction I do not have."

"Sir I am a senior manager of a very big businessman from Ludhiana. He is opening up some big hotels in Lucknow. I am in charge of buying lands and organising everything."

"But you told my son you yourself own hotels in Lucknow?" the prince asked.

No sir, he misunderstood. I had told him that my boss is staying in a big hotel in Lucknow and will be here for a month," the man clarified.

"You haven't yet told me your name; the big businessman who is your boss must also be having a name?"

"I will tell everything as soon as the deal is settled between us," the man said.

"Which deal are you talking about?" the prince asked with obvious anger.

"He told me that he wants to buy something from you," one of the sons intervened.

"And you demented boy, you couldn't tell him that I have nothing left to sell," the prince chided his son and turned towards the suited-booted man, "Gentleman, I would advise you to leave immediately. I have nothing to sell." The prince called out to Baqar Mian who came out from under the thatch with his son who was visiting him. The prince got up and started taking big strides to go into his house. Before Baqar Mian could tell him to leave the man said, "The whole of Lucknow tells me that you have the most precious gem still with you." Then he rushed behind the prince and whispered something in his ears. The next moment the prince sprung around and gave a tight slap on the man's cheek. Baqar Mian and his son asked no questions, just took their master's walking stick and thrashed the suited-booted man till he was reduced to a pulp and then threw him out of the lawn. The two alcoholic sons had also joined Baqar Mian and his son in thrashing the man. But they were not going to be left unpunished.

The prince's wrath was next focussed on his two sons. He used his shoes to beat them. "You shameless men, why did you not drown yourself in the Gomti before bringing such a cheap man into this house? You scoundrels. Have you forgotten the day when you put an abrupt end to your sister's studies at an intensely crucial juncture? All because you thought that it would be the height of '*bepurdagi*' if she at fifteen sat in the same hall with boys writing the same examination. And today you bring a pimp into this house and present him before her father to ask for her? You shameless devils, never show your black faces again."

Their mother had also come out and both of them pushed their two sons out of their house despite their swearing that they had no inkling of the man's evil intentions. "Allah knows that we believed that he wanted to buy gems and that you had some." The boys went on sobbing and begging, but all that the parents said was, "Never enter this place again, not even to lend your shoulders to our dead bodies when we are on our way to the *Qabristan*."

It was a heart-breaking scene that followed. The prince broke down cursing himself for the life that he had led. He realised that he had misused the blessings that Allah had showered upon him. He had misunderstood life totally. He only learnt to take from life but contributed nothing. "This ugly moment which confronted my daughter was a result of my actions and inactions. I don't know how to face my child, what to say to her, how to redeem her life."

Zehra, who was not far from where her father was weeping, was also hysterical. But seeing her father in that condition, she controlled herself, wiped her eyes, covered her head with a *dupatta* and came out with a glass of cold water. She persuaded her father to drink the water. Then she brought more water in a jug along with a basin and washed and wiped his face. She then said, "*Abba Huzoor,* you have already redeemed my life. After your action today, do you think that crook, or anyone with evil intentions, will be seen even miles from this house, never!" Both the parents and Baqar Mian who was standing behind the curtain, burst into tears again.

"Forgive me my child," the prince folded his hands and looked at his daughter. Zehra separated her father's hands and put them with respect on her forehead.

"*Abba Huzoor,*" she said, "Whatever you have done so far has been for my good. I don't doubt your intentions. All you have to do now is to take me back to my old school. I want to continue my studies. Even if a decade has gone by since I last held a book in my hands, so what? Even if I am twenty five years old now, so what?"

And immediately Baqar Mian was told to get a rickshaw to take father and daughter to the convent from where a decade ago Zehra had passed her pre-Senior Cambridge. Both feared that the new nuns and teachers would not recognise them. That Zehra's favourite nun Mother Christopher Michael may have been transferred to another city. These thoughts passed through their minds as both waited in the parlour for Mother Superior. But to their pleasant surprise, it was Mother Christopher Michael who walked in. She recognised Zehra immediately. In the last decade she had been sent to Shillong, Darjeeling and Calcutta. But only a couple of months ago she had been sent back to Lucknow as Mother Superior.

Zehra and her father told Mother Christopher about every detail of their lives including their present penniless condition and the shameful incident that had happened that morning. "Forget about the decade that has gone by my child," Mother Christopher said, "begin life today Zehra. There is still time to fill the High School examination application form. You can appear this very year for the examination and be successful, God willing." The father and daughter were overjoyed but there was a greater joy waiting for them.

"I need a teacher for the lower and middle K.G. and Zehra can take up the job today. The school will pay her a salary of ₹ 120," Mother Christopher announced and Zehra and her father were ecstatic.

In 1960 a family of three could easily have a frugal survival on that amount. They stood before Mother Superior like embodiments of gratitude. They could not find words to thank her.

On their return home Zehra gave the good news to her mother and also from behind the curtain to Baqar Mian, their faithful servant. But there was a promise she took from her parents. "*Abba Huzoor* I want to thank you for allowing me to continue with my studies and for letting me work as a teacher in the convent."

Both her parents blessed her and turned towards the tap for ablutions for a *namaz of shukrana* to Allah. Just then Zehra said, "Before you thank Allah you will have to make a promise to me."

"Go ahead," the father said.

"You and *Ammi Huzoor* will also have to start working," she said.

"*Beta*, where can I go to work? I have never worked before. I will be too embarrassed to ask for work. People will laugh at me and say 'What a strange prince, he works!'"

"Forget that you are a prince and forget that you had money. Haven't you studied law? Refresh your knowledge, go to a lawyer you know, and tell him that you want to work under him," Zehra suggested.

After the thanksgiving namaz, the prince walked to a lawyer who lived opposite Kallan ki Lat and who was his classmate at the Lucknow University. Though the prince had never made an effort to meet the advocate during his happy years this was a happy meeting.

The advocate treated him with tremendous affection and was all encouragement when he heard that the prince wanted to work. He sent back the prince with his *munshi* loaded with big books connected with the Indian Penal Code and Criminal Procedure Code.

When Shehzadi Huzoor saw her husband coming back with a *munshi* and all those books and files she ran to Zehra and said, "If your father can work I will work too. If he can do *vakalat* I can do very good stitching and embroidery."

Before Zehra could respond the prince said, "Why not, go ahead!"

From that day there was a happy and healthy atmosphere in that house. One day Shehzade Huzoor asked, "How is everyone so happy now?"

"*Abba Huzoor*, because we are all working. When one works, one has hope and so one is happy," Zehra said and continued, "If this was not so, Nawab Vazeer Asif-ud-Daulah would have distributed money as charity when the great famine of 1784 occurred and reduced even noblemen and princes to penury. Instead he started building the Great Imambara to create employment for the poor as well as for the high and mighty who had become impoverished". Zehra said.

"You mean even the nobles worked like labour to build the Imambara!" Shehzadi Begum sounded as though she couldn't believe it.

"Yes everyone had to work for the same number of hours and only then they were paid the wages," Zehra explained.

"But everyone was not a trained mason, most of them couldn't have been even experienced labour, then how did they end up building such an excellent masterpiece of architecture?" Shehzadi Begum asked.

"The nawab knew that the work of everyone, particularly the nobles and princes, would not be up to the mark. Such work was pulled down daily and rebuilt by experts. But no one was punished for his bad work nor paid less wages.

The Imambara and Bhul-bhulaiya the maze inside it, took seven years to complete. The expenditure on the whole building was ten million rupees. The intention of the nawab was to show that no work is below anyone's dignity. Dignity of labour as we call it today," Zehra said.

"How has our little child become so wise?" Shehzadi Begum asked, with obvious pride.

While Zehra just smiled back at her mother, Prince Haris Hussain said with all humility, "Don't ask questions just thank Allah for gifting her to us and guiding us onto the right path."

Stop It!

My house opposite Kallan ki Lat European Cemetery was quite a distance from my school. A good forty-minute drive by *Bagghi*, that beautiful Royal-blue one-horse carriage my father bought for me when I was admitted to school. I was in the fourth standard when our horse died. Thereafter it was a rickshaw ride to school. The rickshaw puller took a few minutes less. That's about all. But I always made good use of the time.

When I learned to read, I used all the travel-time reading the sign boards aloud. As the carriage sailed through the almost empty Kachehri Road, Qaiserbagh, Lalbagh, I found boards and boards to read. But beyond that, there were not many. And on the last stretch, from Royal Hotel to Loreto Convent, there were none.

As I grew older I used that time to polish up the lessons which were a part of my homework. The time was used with even better results as I rose in seniority. Soon my studiousness caught the attention of some boys who hung outside their school which was on my way.

Not that they were impressed with my diligence but they were kind of amused. They started passing funny remarks.

One would scream "*Baby ikanni lo kitab do*," another would whistle. Yet another would make faces. There were some who would just make a nuisance of themselves.

I was already twelve years old and fast heading towards my thirteenth birthday. My teachers had started appreciating my conscientiousness. And I was proud of it. This roadside behaviour irritated me. I spoke about it to Veronica, my best friend in school.

"They must be a pack of uncultured scoundrels. Never be scared of them. Just shout back and tell them to 'Stop it', and they will stop the nonsense forever." This was Veronica's advice to me, which I took as a command.

The following day as the rickshaw went past the boys' school and the screeching and screaming began, there was another scream, louder and clearer, bursting from my throat. "Stop it," I said, and stunned the boys into an incredible silence.

But the silence was momentary. As my rickshaw moved, ahead, I heard a chorus of 'Stop it', repeatedly, till my rickshaw turned right at Sarojini Naidu Marg.

And, then, for years, a chorus of "Stop it" greeted me, as my rickshaw passed by the boys' school. Even when I had completed school and entered College, the chorus was there to greet me; only the strength of the chorus had dwindled.

In course of time there was further dwindling of voices. The reduced number of voices became noticeable. Soon there was just one voice left, but loud and clear it was.

This one voice would confront me with a loud "Stop it" anywhere in Lucknow. It was quite natural for me to suddenly turn in the direction of the voice. In that split of a second all that I would be able to see were two amused eyes and a face with a broad grin. That continued for decades. Who was the person behind those amused eyes and broad grin, I never cared to know; and the "voice" never dared to tell.

I completed my studies, joined service, went all over the country obeying the transfer orders of the Government of India; but each time I was back in Lucknow, I would be greeted by a "Stop it," if ever I ventured out of my house. The resounding voice would draw my attention briefly and all that I would notice would be two amused eyes and a broad grin.

Decades later, when I was posted in Allahabad, I came to Lucknow on tour. I was coming back from a meeting in a white Ambassador car with a red siren light making circular movements on the forehead of the vehicle.

As we reached Qaiserbagh Circus and the car negotiated round the fountain, a loud "Stop it" brought the entire traffic to a halt.

Not just my head but many other heads turned in the direction of the resounding voice. I saw a pair of amused eyes and a broad grin greeting me from a face which was no longer young. It was emaciated and tired. He was standing near Anand Cinema and to my great surprise, jumping with joy as he repeatedly shouted "Stop it!"

This was thirty years after I had shouted the two words at the boys standing near the gate of their school, in response to my friend Veronica's advice.

That day I was tempted to turn towards Veronica's house and not towards mine, just to tell her how wrong she was to advise me to shout back at the boys. Veronica laughed her sides out when I told her about the "Stop it" scene at the Qaiserbagh Chauraha.

"Don't forget dear girl," she said, "I was not even thirteen, nor were you, when I gave you that advice. But today I'd say that for the Lucknow-walas even eve-teasing is 'till death do us part."

But this time I took no notice of Veronica's remarks. Both of us laughed light-heartedly and I went back home.

Back in Allahabad, a little more than a month later, I was turning the pages of an Urdu Daily, when I saw two amused eyes staring at me from a photograph in the newspaper. I looked closer, and to my surprise, I saw a familiar broad grin.

I was indeed taken aback. What could this chap have done to earn publicity through a newspaper? I wondered! I read the caption under the photograph. It was an announcement. A *Majlis* was being convened at Lucknow for the person in the photograph on the fortieth day of his death so that relatives and friends could come and pray for his soul to rest in peace.

And Lucknow streets never echoed with a loud resounding "Stop it" again.

The Storm*

It all started when Ganga Din came home drunk and was welcomed with a tight slap by his wife Chunni. Before Ganga Din could react, Chunni was pulled to the ground by Ganga Din's father Sarju and his two wives and their innumerable progeny. All of them combined to give Chunni what she deserved for her unforgivable behaviour. The incident was an unprecedented one; it took no time to reach the ears of everyone who mattered in the *mohalla*. A crowd gathered outside Sarju's *jhuggi* to sympathise with him and his son and to advise them as to what action should be taken to nip the evil in the bud. Some suggested that Chunni should be sent back to her parents and Ganga Din should get a *farkhati*. Such a girl should not be allowed to stay in the locality for, after all, bad habits spread like fire. There were other young girls and daughters-in-law, who could pick up these devilish traits.

"We cannot encourage such independence in our daughters. After all they have to get married and go to another house. The wisdom of a girl lies in her accepting her man's ways and living as he wants her to live," these words of wisdom poured from

* This story has appeared in the *Statesman* on 2 October 1977.

Banvari's lips. Banvari commanded great respect in the entire Sweeper Colony, since he had the coveted job of a sweeper at the Charbagh railway station. It was a government job and one which would provide him a pension, when he was too old to work. But people had other reasons also to respect him. He was a man of principles. And above all, he treated women as they should be treated. He never allowed them to sit on his head, as some of the younger men had the tendency to do. The limp in his wife's leg continued to remind people of this admirable trait in Banvari. Two years ago he beat his wife with a lathi and fractured her ankle bone. Even Makhan *Pahelvan's* massaging could not join the bone which Banvari's lathi had set apart. She had no reason to complain either. After two whole months they were going to have meat in the house and the stupid woman started talking to her neighbour after putting the pan on the fire. She came back only when the meat was charred. Obviously then she had to pay for spoiling the one kilo of meat with her bones.

"Banvari *Bhaiya* is right," Lambo, Sarju's first wife and Ganga Din's mother agreed. Looking at Sarju she said, "Go and push her into the hell she has come from; there is no place for her in this house." But Banvari stepped in again. "Sending Chunni away will solve the problem only partially. It is the source of the evil which should be attacked if the evil has to be banished. Chunni was not born with these habits, she picked them up from someone, and I can guarantee that she has learnt these habits from this very neighbourhood." Everyone knew that Banvari was hinting at Ghengaran, who had come to live in this colony with her husband and large family and one other man, a couple of years ago. The entire crowd found in Banvari's words a reflection of their own ideas. They had resented Ghengaran's stay in their colony from the very beginning, not because she hailed from another part of Lucknow, but because of her strange ways. She was a peculiar woman indeed, the only one of her kind on the face of the globe. She lived openly with two men, her husband and her childhood paramour Girdhari, who was not even a sweeper by caste. For her wild ways everyone blamed her husband. The shameless wretch knew what was happening in his house but preferred to look the other way. As for Girdhari, no one in the entire Kallan ki Lat Sweeper Colony, could reason as to what he saw in that dark, ugly, middle aged woman, with a large goitre on her neck. It was the goitre that gave her the name Ghengaran, (*Ghenga* is Hindi for goitre). One could only laugh to think that for this sharp tongued ugly woman, Girdhari had left his home and *biradari* and taken to pulling a rickshaw for a livelihood. He lived openly with Ghengaran, gave her a ten-rupee note every day as well as a breakfast of jalebi and milk. And God forbid, if ever there was one jalebi less for breakfast or one paisa less in the daily allowance. The whole *mohalla* was witness to the beating which Girdhari was subjected to on such occasions. It was indeed surprising how Girdhari never thought of paying her back in her own coin. He would only ask for mercy while uttering endearments. It was invariably her husband who would plead Girdhari's case, as Girdhari would, his, when Ghengaran's temper was focussed on her husband. Obviously the people who lived around saw ugliness in this strange understanding amongst the trio. They spoke against her behind her back, but no one could ever dare to question her on her life.

At this moment, when Banvari's words shifted the attention of the crowd from Chunni to Ghengaran, she was sitting on her large cot, as though the whole world belonged to her. The cot was half in her veranda and half on the road balancing itself over the drain in which her little son Ghaseete had just eased himself. Ghengaran was eating chaat from a large leaf. She knew what had happened at her neighbour Sarju's, but she was not one who would ever waste time involving herself in other people's affairs! But suddenly she saw the crowd pushing towards her *jhuggi* and soon the elders among them had surrounded her cot. Her husband sensed the danger; he mingled with the crowd and disappeared. Girdhari preferred to stand by the side of his mistress like a faithful dog. Ghengaran too smelt seriousness in the atmosphere. But by now she had faced many such crowds. The *mohalla* where she lived earlier had also given her similar threats. But she had left that house only when she had wanted. At this moment also, not a trace of nervousness touched her ebony face. She continued to eat the chaat with as much gusto as she did before, while the crowd watched her slipping one *golgappa* after another into her mouth. The *golgappas* all devoured, it was the turn of the leaf which was acting as a plate. Only after licking the leaf clean did she address the people, "What is it that you want?" her voice shrill but oozing with confidence. Half the crowd thought it wise to disperse. Some played it safe by standing at a distance. But Sarju and Banvari had the do-or-die look on their faces. Banvari had to prove that he could never be scared of a woman. Sarju and his family were of course the aggrieved.

"Look Ghengaran, you will have to leave our *mohalla*, we cannot have a woman like you in Kallan ki Lat."

"Kallan ki Lat is not your father's *jagir*. I shall not leave." On such occasions Ghengaran preferred to be brief.

"Then we'll call a panchayat."

"Do as you please."

"We want to know who this man is," Sarju said, pointing towards Girdhari, "what is your relationship with him?"

"Yes we want to know," echoed the crowd.

Now this was asking for trouble. They should have been thankful that Ghengaran had been rather decent with them, as far as her language was concerned. Her normal speech was strewn with a variety of four letter words. "*Haramiyon*," Ghengaran preferred to use the plural, for she did not want to spare anyone in the crowd. Her sharp eyes swept over every face in the gathering and then rested on the vocal leaders, "Who conferred upon you the right to ask me that question? Go to your father, the Sarpanch, and tell him to ask me that question, if he dares to."

The crowd could not stand the fire from Ghengaran's eyes. They started dispersing. Even Sarju and Banvari left. But a panchayat was called and Ghengaran did attend it. A volley of questions was shot at her and she answered each one of them unnerved. Finally the verdict of the *panchas* came, "You will have to throw Girdhari out, and have nothing to do with him."

"I shall not do it," Ghengaran was firm.

"Then you shall have to leave your husband," was the alternative offered.

"I shall not do that either, I have explained before. My husband has no place to go to, his health is failing him, he'll never be able to find shelter," Ghengaran gave her reasons for not accepting the second alternative.

"Then you'll not be allowed to share *hukka pani* with this *biradari*, you are excommunicated. One woman cannot live with two men. Moreover, a woman who beats her husband should be treated like a leper by this society." The panchayat's verdict was final.

Ghengaran was rather happy to have nothing to do with the community which had done nothing good for her, but she decided to ask a parting question.

"Sarpanch Ji, when are you excommunicating Sarju? Hasn't he also got two wives? What is more, both of them are sisters. And doesn't he beat them up whenever he likes?"

The community and the *panchas* were outraged at the woman's impertinence.

"If you do not understand such a simple fact of life, then you don't deserve to live. Sarju has committed no sin, because he is a man. And then every man can correct his woman by scolding or beating her, if she needs correction," Sarpanch Ji explained.

"And men do not need any correction?" Ghengaran asked.

"Yes, they do, sometimes, but not from women."

"Why?" This one word from Ghengaran's mouth echoed and re-echoed. Even the atmosphere seemed desperate to hear the reply. But the sarpanch was not going to answer silly questions put in by dirty women. The *panchas* started packing up. Some of the elders also encouraged them to wind up.

"Is that a question? Sarpanch Sahib cannot waste time over such frivolous questions," Banvari chided Ghengaran.

But in the last five minutes there had been a stir among the ill-clad womenfolk who were standing at a distance. And suddenly a frail voice rose from among the group.

"Don't get ready to go *Huzoor*, you have to do justice in my case. I want to know why Sarju should have beaten me every day. Why did he bring in another wife? He married my own sister. Why wasn't he ever punished? Why?" This *why* was from Sarju's first wife Lambo. She was addressing the sarpanch from behind her *ghunghat*. There followed such a commotion among the men. Even Sarju and Banvari started getting palpitations. A commotion like this was never witnessed in Kallan ki Lat Sweeper Colony, perhaps never in Lucknow. It was as though a storm was going to come.

Or had the storm already come!

Bhagtin

Bhagtin was neither a *Sadhvi*, an ascetic, nor a devotee of any saint. She was the wife of an old potter who was a *bhagat*. The names which their parents gave them were long forgotten. No one cared to know them. People found Bhagat and Bhagtin good enough names for addressing them. They lived in Mohsin Mian's compound which spread between Kallan ki Lat and Kachcha Hata. The rent for the mud house where they lived was four *annas* a month, which they never paid. But they reached Mohsin Mian's *deorhi* religiously at the end of every month, and sat patiently at the gate till the landlord came out, hookah in hand, followed by a servant or two. The couple would then fall at his feet and beg him to exempt them from paying that month's rent. They would cry and rant, mumble something about how they had been starving for want of money.

Mohsin Mian would hear them for a while and then ask, "Will you pay rent from next month?"

"*Jaroor Huzoor jaroor, bhagwan kasam jaroor*," was invariably their answer.

"All right go now," Mohsin Mian would finally tell them.

These words meant that they need not pay rent for that month.

This had been happening for thirty years ever since Bhagat and Bhagtin had come to live in his compound. Mohsin Mian knew from day one that they were never going to pay rent. But he didn't care. What he appreciated was their coming to him every month, to apologise for not paying and to ask for his forgiveness.

Bhagat did nothing for a living. Once in a while he was called to do "*Jharh-Phoonk*," a kind of ritual to cure jaundice patients or those possessed by evil spirits. He charged no money from such patients for that, he believed, would take away his healing powers. But Bhagtin worked in Vakeel Sahib's house to keep her kitchen fire burning. She winnowed the wheat and other food grains, washed and dried them and got them grounded at the watermill. She grounded the grain, for the horse, herself at the stone grinder dug into the floor of Vakeel Sahib's large kitchen. But never did she touch any cooked food from their kitchen or water from their pitcher, though she did the daily shopping of vegetables and meat for the family. She was no vegetarian, though, Bhagat was. In fact she could spend hours sitting at Ishaaq Butcher's shop. For most women of her class, Ishaaq had a strange charm. His fair skin and generosity made them his fans. Once in a while Bhagtin, like other women servants of the locality, got from him a free packet of meat, to carry home.

Bhagtin's work at Vakeel Sahib's house was completed early in the day. She spent the rest of the day time cutting betel nuts for a shopkeeper in Fatehganj. The shopkeeper's servant delivered a *seer* of *supari* at Bhagtin's house and took it back after she had cut them into fine, even, and equal pieces. She was given two *annas* and four uncut suparis for her pains. The work took three full days to complete. Obviously Bhagtin found supari cutting very difficult and hazardous. The shopkeeper showed no consideration, if she injured her fingers, which she often did, despite her expertise and her sharp-bladed *sarauta*.

But Bhagtin did not give up the work. She was not used to sitting idle and she needed money desperately. If this work was harsh, work at Vakeel Sahib's was very light and his begum was a prompt paymaster. Bhagtin felt compensated. Above all, she never had to bother about clothes. Once or twice a year, she got an old saree and blouse from Begum Sahib for herself and an old shirt for Bhagat. The saree was long enough to cover her upper body and head too. She had long given up wearing a blouse. She was too old to bother about those details. Begum Sahib's blouses were too big for her. They were actually *kurtis* which did better as tops over *lehngas* for her twelve-year-old granddaughter Munni. But Begum Sahib had often chided her and explained that it was indecent not to wear a blouse, even if her whole body was covered with the saree. An unstitched material like a saree could uncover her if the wind blew in the wrong direction. Bhagtin started wearing a blouse only when Begum Sahib stitched one for her after taking her measurements. Her husband Bhagat, never felt the harshness of Lucknow winters, for he got Vakeel Sahib's discarded *shalukas*, almost every year, and once in a couple of years, also a *dulai*, which he gave to his wife to use as a shawl.

Why then, did Bhagtin need money desperately? Her motherless granddaughter Munni was about to reach marriageable age and she was left with no resources for the marriage. Bhagtin had divided her quarter *seer* worth of silver ornaments into two equal parts, and given them to her daughter Ramkali and son Jagannath at their weddings. There were no ornaments for Munni, no pots and pans and no money for her trousseau. Munni, was Bhagtin's daughter Ramkali's child, Ramkali had passed away minutes after delivering Munni and Bhagtin had brought the child up with no help from anywhere. Even Munni's father never turned up to enquire about her. The last Bhagtin saw him was at Ramkali's funeral.

Bhagtin saw in Munni Ramkali's reflection. What she could not give to her unfortunate daughter, she wanted to give to Munni. But there was no ray of hope, least of all from her son Jagannath's direction. Jagannath could have helped his mother, if he wanted. He was a railway employee and earned a stable salary, along with a sufficient supply of grains and other food items. Bhagtin was sure, his wife would never let him part with a *paisa* for Munni's wedding. He hadn't spoken to her for years nor had his wife, although they lived very close to each other. So Bhagtin struggled alone.

As a child Jagannath was so different. He was obedient, god-fearing and religious. At eight he told his mother that he wanted to go to Hanuman Mandir in Aliganj, on Bara Mangal, doing the difficult *paikarma* more difficult from the usual circumambulation on one's feet. Bhagtin was ecstatic. She hugged her child and said, "Not till you are fifteen, and then your father and I will walk with you while you do the *paikarma*. I will carry a large jug of iced lemon sherbet for you to sip whenever you are thirsty. Your father will keep throwing buckets full of water on the road, so that my dear child's precious body does not feel the heat."

At fifteen the determined lad completed that long *paikarma* journey to Aliganj Hanuman Mandir on a swelteringly hot May day. His body was bruised but not his spirits. On his return, Bhagtin took him first to Vakeel Sahib's house before she allowed him to cross her threshold. A lot of people had gathered there, to welcome him. He was a pilgrim after all. Vakeel Sahib put a thick garland of *bela* flowers round his neck, gave him his blessings and a ten-rupee note, which left the people awestruck. Even Bhagtin had not received, till then, a note of that denomination.

Vakeel Sahib said that the boy deserved more, and asked him to spend the money as he liked. But a greater surprise awaited the people, who had gathered to welcome him, when the boy said, "I will not spend it; Amma will use it as she wants." For Bhagtin it was a moment of supreme glory. She stood drenched in pride and speechless.

And then Begum Sahib sent a one-rupee coin, with the King's image on it, and a message that he should buy for himself whatever he wanted. Jagannath said excitedly, "No, I only need four *annas*. Three *annas* for *kankaiya* and *dor* and one *anna* for lots of jalebis." Everyone around looked at the fifteen-year-old lad with pride and admiration.

Bhagtin was a lucky mother. Like Jagannath, his elder sister Ramkali was as obedient and affectionate. She never made demands, never grumbled, never sulked. In days of scarcity she would give her share of the meagre meal to her brother and pretend that she was not hungry. But one day, strangely enough, she told her mother that she wanted to wear gold earrings. "Amma, get me gold earrings." Bhagtin was in the midst of a severe financial crisis. She hadn't yet landed that job at Vakeel Sahib's place. Till then he had not moved into the neighbourhood. She flew into a rage and said something which she regretted all her life. "It is difficult for me to fill that fathomless well inside your stomach and you want gold earrings. I'll be surprised if you ever get to wear an ornament made of *raanga*". Ramkali froze. Never again did she open her to mouth to express any wish!

Bhagtin realised immediately that she had uttered unfair and cruel words to an innocent child who had always denied herself. And who perhaps may not have known that gold was not a metal which the poor like her parents could buy for their children. Bhagtin's remorse knew no bounds. She wanted to make up for the unhappiness she had caused the child. She started working harder to save more. All she wanted was to buy a pair of gold earrings for the child. She thought she would be successful in doing so, by the time Ramkali got married. But it was not to be. At her wedding, Ramkali got her share of the silver ornaments and a promise from her mother that soon the gold earrings would follow. Within a year Ramkali was pregnant. By then Bhagtin had saved a substantial amount of money for the earrings, and was sure that she would be able to buy them for her dear daughter by the time she delivered her first child. But that was also not to be. Some complications developed in her pregnancy and Ramkali closed her eyes forever after delivering Munni prematurely. Bhagtin was devastated. But little Munni helped to revive her, by turning her attention all to herself.

Time moved on and Munni reached marriageable age. By the time Bhagat found a groom for her, Bhagtin had collected all that she wanted to give her, including the pair of gold earrings which

had evaded her mother Ramkali. Munni got a husband who was
no ordinary potter. He made mud toys and fruits which could
be mistaken for real ones. At Diwali he was a rich man. But his
wealth never reached Munni's hands. He spent it on clothes and
friends and drinks. He himself dressed like a nawab, and left
Munni to be satisfied with Begum Sahib's old sarees. Bhagtin
and Munni had agreed to keep the silver ornaments and gold
earrings in Begum Sahib's safe custody. They did not think any
valuables were safe in Munni's house with her husband, Madan,
around. He was an incorrigible spendthrift.

Eight years Munni's valuables lay in safe hands, till Vakeel
Sahib decided to go to Pakistan with his family for a month,
during the children's Christmas holidays. Begum Sahib returned
the valuables to Bhagtin promising to take them back on her
return. Bhagtin agreed. Her house, she thought, was safe enough
though she lived there by herself. Bhagat had passed away a
year earlier.

Vakeel Sahib's family had hardly left Lucknow when
Jagannath and Sundaria his wife landed at Bhagtin's house and
fell at her feet, sobbing and wailing. The landlord had turned
them out of their house. The children were sitting on the road.
Bhagtin's heart melted. She ran to fetch the children. "This is
your house my child, never again let tears come into your eyes,"
she said to Jagannath and gave him the only little room that she
had. She moved under the thatched space in the open on that
cold December night, with her tin box in which she had kept
Munni's ornaments.

Sundaria started life at Bhagtin's by doing everything which
she thought would please her. Bhagtin was suspicious and

yet she wanted to believe that there was truth and affection in Sundaria's words and actions. Bhagtin was still swinging between trust and suspicion, when one day she took out the pouch containing the ornaments, hid it in her saree and moved out. She intended to go to Munni's house and hand her the ornaments. Sundaria had seen Bhagtin hide something under her saree.

"Amma, where are you going?" She asked Bhagtin.

"To see Munni," Bhagtin replied.

"Here take some, pooris and halwa for her. I made them for your son this morning." Bhagtin was indeed happy. She turned back, and stretched her hands to take the delicacies from her daughter-in-law. The pouch containing the ornaments fell.

"What is this Amma?" Sundaria asked innocently.

"Munni's ornaments. I was going to give them to her," Bhagtin replied with some nervousness.

"Don't take them with you. Call Munni here, and then give them to her. Luckily the pouch fell in the house. Supposing it had fallen on the road, you would never have found it." Sundaria said all that so convincingly that Bhagtin heard sincerity in her voice. "You lock up the pouch in your box and then go, if you want. If you trust me you can leave it with me instead." Sundaria left Bhagtin with no option but to leave the pouch with her. Had she locked it in the tin box, it would have meant that she did not trust her daughter-in-law.

Munni's house was just a stone's throw from Bhagtin's house, she returned with Munni in a matter of minutes. But the inevitable happened. Sundaria denied that any pouch was left with her, or that she had even seen it. Bhagtin lost her mind.

She begged Sundaria to give it back; she threatened to call the police. People from the neighbourhood intervened. But Sundaria did not budge.

The worst happened when Jagannath came back from work and Bhagtin told him that Sundaria had taken Munni's ornaments. "Munni's ornaments? Where did she get them from?" Jagannath asked most casually.

"I gave them to her at her wedding," Bhagtin said, weeping all the while.

"What right have you to give anything to Munni?" Jagannath had the audacity to say.

"They were bought with my hard earned money." Bhagtin said with anger.

"So what? If there is anyone who has a right to your hard earned money, it is me, your son. The ornaments have gone to the right place. Stop crying. Go to sleep." Jagannath's tone sounded like a court verdict. Bhagtin was shattered. She fell on her cot never to get up again. With every day that passed, her condition deteriorated, and she kept on asking for Vakeel Sahib and Begum Sahib. Munni was also counting the days for their return. Jagannath did not cease to be cruel to his mother, even when she was so near death. "They did not go there to come back. Who comes back from Pakistan?" Jaggannath said, and Bhagtin started weeping inconsolably.

But Vakeel Sahib and his family did come back. They rushed to see her, as soon as they heard the entire story from Munni. But before that, Vakeel Sahib called Jagannath to his house. He ordered him to give back the jewellery to his mother. At first Jagannath denied knowing anything about it but when

Vakeel Sahib said he will send the police to take him in for interrogation to the police station, and have him kept there as long as the rules require, and also to have suspension orders issued, if necessary, terminating his services from the Railways, Jagannath fell at his feet, and promised to give back the jewellery within an hour. And he did.

On seeing Vakeel Sahib and his wife Bhagtin got some semblance of life on her face. She started talking. She cursed herself for having kept Jagannath in her womb and delivering him to the world. But she would not defile herself any further. She did not want Jagannath and his family to even touch her dead body; she forbade him to perform her last rites. She wanted Vakeel Sahib to give *agni* to her dead body. All present were taken aback, most of all Vakeel Sahib. He decided to divert Bhagtin's mind to pleasant thoughts. "But first take this pouch which Jagannath has brought back," he cajoled. Bhagtin took the pouch in her hands, checked the ornaments and gave them to Munni. She looked overjoyed, and continued to talk. She said that Vakeel Sahib had given her more happiness than anyone else could have done. She led a very happy and respectable life after she got to know him more than twenty-five years ago. She looked at Vakeel Sahib and said, "You will have to promise me that you will give *agni* to my mortal remains."

"What are you saying Bhagtin," Vakeel Sahib said, "You are not going to die yet. You will live to be hundred years, *Insha Allah.*" Bhagtin smiled, held his hand, and crossed over to the other world.

That evening, in Bhaisakund Crematorium, there was a strange sight. Syed Mohammad Usman, advocate, was performing the last rites of Jagrani Kumharan better known as Bhagtin.

And that was not very long ago. The year was Nineteen Hundred and Sixty.

Never Fool a Woman

It was a humid July night. The time was moving towards midnight. After prolonged arguments she went into the house and re-entered the drawing room with the family's double-barrelled gun and shot at him just when he had reached the door to leave. She shot again to make sure that he didn't escape. Her target was right. He fell at the door. His body was sprawled half inside and half outside the drawing room. His Vespa, painted brown, on which he had come to her house, stood a couple of feet away from the drawing room under the open sky. Her house had no boundary walls and no hedges. From outside people could see the activities in the outer rooms of the house, if the curtains were not drawn.

The gunshot surprised those who were still awake, and woke up those who had gone off to sleep. Soon the mohalla was abuzz. People started moving in the direction of the sound of the gunshot. A dhobhi, who was still at work, a little distance from her house, ironing clothes in the light of a lantern, turned his head with a jerk towards the house, and through the open door saw her with the gun in her hands. The Police found in the dhobhi the only eyewitness to the murder, for there was no one in the drawing room when she fired. Lucknow had witnessed many a brave woman fire at men when its independence was in danger, but, for the first time ever, saw a woman shooting her unfaithful lover! Obviously then, that gunshot sounded the end of that woman's anonymity and privacy.

Thereafter, life took her through another course altogether, where she came face to face with only policemen, journalists and lawyers. She never saw home again, but only prison cells and courtrooms; never met friends but crowds who climbed walls and trees, desperate to have just one look at her, a mere glimpse. There was no dearth of direct and circumstantial evidence against her. She was convicted at every level of the judiciary. Her mercy petition to the president was granted, no doubt, but after she had already spent seven years behind bars, much to her own disgrace and that of her family. The simple girl, who had nothing in her to make her stand out as different from the rest, became the most written about, the most talked about and the most photographed woman of her times.

It was this woman whom I met more than forty years later when she came looking for a job to the school I was running in Lucknow. She was above sixty then, had never taught in a school before, but had given private tuitions to children at home. I tried to explain that no one begins a career at that age, but all in vain. She was desperate to get a job. For reasons not even known to myself, I obliged, but on condition that her work was found satisfactory. She agreed. I never found her wanting. In fact she was willing to take on more and more responsibility.

When I gave her the job in the school I did not know who she was, but after she had proved her competence she disclosed her identity. I was taken aback, and quite angry with her for concealing such important facts of her life from me. I withdrew her services from the school immediately, but didn't have the heart to deprive her of her bread and butter. I put her on my private computer to type the book I was writing. Much to my surprise, unlike women of her age, she was good at the computer. In course of time she volunteered to tell me her story.

After her release from prison, her family didn't allow her to live in Lucknow, so she moved to Delhi, into her elder brother's house. Her parents also lived in the same house. Her brother gave her a new name and insisted that she be called by that name.

"You will not go by the name which brought disgrace to you and our family. For me, the girl who bore that name died long ago. I don't want my children to hear that name or to know that girl." Then, putting his hand on her head, he said, "This is my sister Amina, she is born today."

Since that day no one ever called her by her original name. Even her parents called her Amina. Her brother's children had seen her for the first time. They knew her as Aunt Amina from Lucknow. She was not allowed to venture out of the house unaccompanied and without a burqa. She also preferred to remain indoors for fear of the media which still pursued her. But as time moved on the media gave up. The number of people who recognised her dwindled, and now, forty-two years later, there were few who remembered the story of the girl who shot her lover for infidelity.

Amina told me that she met Dr Siddharth in the Government Hospital in Lucknow where her father was admitted after a stroke. He was a neurologist who treated her father and was known for his correct diagnosis and expertise. He was above thirty-five years then, while Amina was still a teenager, a student of BSc, just about to celebrate her twentieth birthday. So long as her father was in the hospital, she remained by his side for most of the day till her brother Ehsan came in the evening to relieve her. Ehsan would then help her get a rickshaw to reach home. One day the two of them were standing at the hospital gate with no rickshaw in sight. It was quite late in the evening. They looked worried. Suddenly a scooter stopped. The rider was the neurologist who was attending on their father. "What is the matter?" he asked.

"We are looking for a rickshaw for my sister to go back home," Ehsan said.

The doctor parked his scooter near the gate and came to where the siblings were standing. "Come, and let's walk up to the Charbatti Chauraha, we are sure to get a rickshaw there."

"No Doctor Sahib, we will go ourselves," Ehsan said.

"Come come, I'll walk with you," the doctor insisted.

They had hardly walked a few steps when a rickshaw, coming from the opposite direction, stopped in front of them.

"Why are you walking *Daakter* Sahib, rickshaw *hazir hai*." The rickshawala addressed the doctor with all the courtesy he could gather. Apparently Dr Siddharth was well known in that area and very popular among the poor whom he attended to with compassion. He told the rickshawala to reach the girl to her house and paid him the fare in advance. Amina and Ehsan felt highly obliged.

Their father remained in the hospital for a whole month, during which time Dr Siddharth won the family's respect and total trust. They were impressed with his courteous behaviour and the care and concern he showed to his patient. As for Amina, she had developed quite a soft spot for him, by the time her father was discharged. In the presence of others, the doctor praised Amina for being a dutiful daughter. When he found her alone, he showered her with compliments. He would tell her that she was different from all other women that he had met. Ultimately he started telling her that she had lent a new meaning to his life. How he wished he had met her earlier!

The doctor continued to visit Amina's home even after her father was discharged from the hospital. In fact he attended to anyone who fell ill in the family or anyone recommended by them. His name became a household word in the family. But Dr Siddharth's concentration was on Amina. From verbal compliments he slowly graduated to typing out small notes with Urdu couplets and quietly handing them to her. Soon the love notes became longer, long enough to be letters–typed and unsigned.

Amina was swept off her feet. Her thoughts started revolving solely round the doctor. She could see only good qualities in him. She found herself willing to obey his word like a command. Soon they started seeing each other. Often she would miss college and go to meet him. Not long after he offered to divorce his wife to marry her. He begged her to let him have a couple of more years to earn enough through his private practice so that he could give a proper allowance to his wife and children, at the time of divorce. Amina was on the top of the world. She was willing to wait as long as he wanted. There was nothing she was not ready to do to have him all to herself. He made her believe that no woman in the world was loved as much as he loved her—a belief which was enough to boost a young girl's confidence and transform it into arrogance.

Soon the family guessed what was happening between Amina and Dr Siddharth. They showed their disapproval and tried to wean her away from the unhealthy liaison. Amina took no notice of the warning given by her parents. On the contrary she threatened to walk out if they put any pressure on her. After giving her parents this ultimatum, Amina headed towards their meeting place. It was a cosy little room, near the hospital, which the doctor had hired. Though it was not their scheduled meeting time, she just wanted to be by herself, away from her family. But the doctor was there. She was surprised but extremely relieved to find him.

"How are you here at this time?" she asked.

"My heart told me that my little angel needs me at this hour," he answered. And Amina told him all that had happened at home. The doctor advised her, never to lose her temper with her parents and brothers. "You should remain cool till all obstacles to our marriage are removed." He was so gentle and caring that all tensions and fears vanished from her mind and she felt as light as a feather. When she got up to go back, her eyes, suddenly, stopped at a pretty pink ladies' handkerchief lying on the floor near the table. "Whose hanky is this?" she asked.

For a split second, the doctor looked pale, but recovered immediately, and said, "*Meri Jaan*, it is yours, you must have forgotten it on one of your visits." And Amina remembered that twelve beautiful pink ladies' handkerchiefs were presented to her by the doctor in a velvet box on her last birthday and she had been using them. She picked it up to keep it in her purse. The doctor snatched it away, and said, "No, this hanky is mine now." She let him have it and left in a cheerful mood.

But the episode of the pink handkerchief did not end there. One day while cleaning her almirah, Amina found the beautiful velvet box in which the twelve handkerchiefs were given to her. She took them out from the box, to touch them again. Looking at them and feeling them gave her a strange pleasure. She had been using those hankies no doubt, but she would wash them, iron them, and keep them in the box. Unintentionally she started counting them. She found all twelve intact. She counted them over and over again and each time she ended up with the figure twelve.

That day when she met him, she was full of joy as usual. "You know there must have been thirteen hankies in the lovely velvet box you gave me. The suppliers must have packed an extra hanky into the box," she said, oozing enthusiasm.

"Is that so?" the doctor said, doubtfully, trying to read the reaction on her face. Seeing no guile or sarcasm there, emboldened, he ventured, "Oh! Then perhaps, the packers knew that the prettiest girl on earth was going to use them. Pretty girls deserve more of everything! You see!" he said, complimenting her as always, not realising then that the pink hankies would keep surfacing in his life over and over again and finally would tie themselves up into a rope to hang him.

Amina soon realised that her velvet box had only twelve pink hankies and not thirteen as she had presumed in her innocence when, on a Saturday morning, she went to the Mayfair building to look for a book in the British Council Library. Exactly at noon she finished with her work in the library and came down. There was a crowd in the lobby. The morning show in the Mayfair cinema hall had just ended and people were coming out of the hall. Amina decided to wait on the steps of the library for the crowd to disperse. Suddenly she saw the doctor on the exit steps of the balcony. He was not alone. A lady, who was definitely not his wife, was with him. Amina knew his wife as she had seen her earlier. This lady was definitely not his wife! She waited for the doctor to descend the steps and leave the lobby. Then she followed them and saw the lady go with him on his brown Vespa. Before the lady sat on the pillion with her arms round his waist, she tied her short but unruly hair with a *familiar pink hanky*.

Amina was shattered; she had no memories of how she reached home. She didn't dare to tell anyone what had happened, for each one in the family had been repeatedly telling her that she was pursuing the wrong person. But in an hour's time she was drugging herself with a consoling explanation, "Maybe she was his sister or his cousin, and he has every right to take her for an outing, and why can't he give his sister the same present as he gives me?" Amina's mind was weaving excuses on behalf of the doctor, hypnotising herself. In an hour or two, in a miraculous way, she got the strength to get up and walk in the direction of their meeting place. She found the room bolted from inside, which meant that the doctor was there. Only she and the doctor had the keys to the room. She rang the bell, she knocked, she called but, the door was not opened to her. She waited several hours before she decided to leave. Just then the elderly landlady who lived on the first floor, called out to her. Amina went in.

"Are you a patient of the doctor? I see you very often going into the room," the landlady asked Amina. She had no answer.

"Whoever you are," the landlady continued, "I must inform you that a number of young ladies go into the room when the doctor is in, and come out after hours. Even now there is a lady inside the room with him. I saw both of them go in together. When he hired the room, he told me that he was writing his thesis and needed to be by himself, in a secluded place."

The landlady looked at Amina, she waited for her to say something. When Amina kept quiet, the landlady looked at her with sympathy and said, "And you my girl, you look at least ten to fifteen years younger than him. My advice to you is, stay away from him." Amina broke down. She had to be put on a rickshaw by the landlady and sent back home.

Thereafter for more than a week Amina kept on trying to contact the doctor but was not able to reach him. Then suddenly one day he came on the line. He told Amina that he was down with flu. Amina remained cool, and called him over to her house. He promised to come in the evening. But he arrived after ten and made profuse apologies for a late entry. He spoke at length to Amina's father about his health, and prescribed a few tonics for him.

Then Amina came into the drawing room. He searched for anger on her face, but found her quite normal. She was in total control of herself. She wanted to have a word with him alone.

"Doctor Sahib," she said, "I have been ringing you up for over a week. Remember, I requested you to help me fill up the form for this year's Pre-Medical Test."

"Oh Sure," the doctor replied, and then turning to her father he said, "Your daughter, sir, wants to become a doctor."

"She will have to work very hard for that," her father responded.

Her mother said with a lot of affection, "She can never become a surgeon. She is so soft-hearted. She faints at the sight of blood." That was a mother's assessment of a daughter who was, in a short time from then, going to kill the man she loved! The father and mother came out of the room to allow their daughter to fill up her Pre-Medical Test form. Both parents thought, much to their relief, that their daughter was consciously directing her attention towards a more constructive road, and was staying away from the one she had strayed into. While coming out of the drawing room, the father said, "Didn't I tell you, my daughter will soon be on the right path!"

The mother smiled hopefully.

The scene in the drawing room was not what the parents thought and hoped it would be. The two sat across a table with the Pre-Medical Test form, no doubt, placed on the table, but their conversation did not even hover around the form. Amina confronted the doctor with all that she had seen and experienced in the last ten days. He looked unfazed. Yes he was in the room that afternoon, but alone and in deep slumber. He could not have heard when she called at the door.

The night before, he had an emergency which kept him awake. He was very tired, the morning after, and thought he would not get total rest at home, and so decided to go to their room to sleep. The landlady's accusations too, the doctor demolished. "Never believe the old lady," he said, "she wants to get the room vacated, as she needs it now." His visit to Mayfair with the young lady was totally denied by him. When Amina said that she saw them there "with her own eyes," and described how the lady sat on the pillion of his Vespa, he said, "I have no explanation for your hallucinations."

Amina would have taken his words for truth, had he not denied his visit to the Mayfair Cinema. She was willing to cajole herself to believe that he was fast asleep when she knocked at the door, but how could she disbelieve her own eyes for what they had seen at the Mayfair Cinema. Amina had blindly trusted him till that very hour. In fact she had been finding excuses for him to satisfy herself. How could he accuse her of having hallucinations? He had betrayed her trust. She felt cheated by someone whom she thought was her only pillar of strength. In a state of sheer helplessness, she dissolved into tears. The doctor got up in a fit of anger, and said, "If you do not trust me, you can break off with me this minute." He banged his fist on the table. Amina felt her world collapsing. For once she failed to put her reactions into words. But the doctor was quite easy with his utterances. "I loved you not only with all my heart, but with my soul, but now I am better off without you," he said, standing up. Amina could feel deceit pouring from his voice. She got up from her chair and walked out of the drawing room. He saw her go in, and then turned towards the door to leave.

But Amina was back within seconds, this time, with a gun. She was determined not to let him make his exit from her door. And exit he did not. Not alive. It was his body which left her house, many hours later, policemen carrying it on their shoulders!

The story of Amina left me with a lot of questions. I wondered whether she regretted killing her lover. "No," was her firm answer. "I have no regrets, in fact I am happy because had he lived he would have spoiled the lives of some more young and gullible girls after leading them astray with his charms. But," she added, "I do regret spoiling my life and that of my parents and siblings. Had I not used the gun, I would have spared myself and my family the trauma, which became our destiny." She stopped and appeared drowned in her thoughts. Then suddenly she continued, "And I also believe, had I not used the gun on him, when I did, I would have continued to fool myself about his good intentions, and ended up with a life worse than what it is today. It would have been a life despised by all, including myself."

"I got the impression through your narrative that he was very compassionate and a good doctor," I said.

"Yes, that he was," she said. "He handled his patients with compassion and care, he was very duty conscious as a doctor but…" she stopped midway.

"But what?" I prodded.

"The good man transformed into a villain when it came to women; he charmed them into submission, and then dismissed them with contempt as his conquests." She summed up his character. After some thought she added, "He may have deserved bouquets as a doctor, I agree, but for treating women as he did, he deserved what he got from me." That last sentence left her lips wrapped in fire. I was overawed. I thought I saw in her burning eyes the same conviction which must have sparked in them, forty-two years earlier, when she picked up the gun, and fired at the man she loved.

Qudsia Begum*

"Sabiha," Qudsia Begum almost screamed at Vakeel Sahib's daughter who was so taken aback that she dropped the knitting needles from her hands and took some time to regain her composure. And when she did, she looked questioningly at Qudsia Begum.

"What did I do? Why did you get so angry *Apa*?" Sabiha was perplexed.

Sabiha was doing her BA from a local college and lived in a large house in the next lane. She would drop in quite often to pick up a knitting pattern or to learn some embroidery. Qudsia Begum too would visit her on her holidays. Sabiha's parents were very fond of her and respected her. There were three girls and a boy in that family. Sabiha being the eldest among the girls exercised considerable influence in the family.

But what was it that made the calm and composed Qudsia Begum lose her cool. It is true that ever since Arshad Mian had married a girl who had been studying with him, without his parent's approval, Sabiha had been talking of nothing but her brother's *bad taste*. Today again she had been telling the

* This story appeared in the *Hindustan Times* Weekly Sunday 28 August 1977.

older woman how dark and unattractive her sister-in-law was. Sabiha found it difficult to understand how her brother, who was otherwise so obedient, could keep his parents in the dark about such an important matter. After all he was aware that *Ammi* and *Abba* had given their word to Justice Ikramuddin, whose daughter was as beautiful as the moon. Even if he did not want to marry her he could have at least married a girl from a decent background. Sabiha said she shuddered to think how her father would face his colleagues at the *kachehri*. People would soon get to know that his son had married the daughter of a *peshkar*, a low court official. Poor Vakeel Sahib! With his roaring practice and place in society, he had dreams of becoming a judge. The whole of Lucknow will now laugh at him. Qudsia Begum was listening to all this without any comment. She continued to iron her heavily starched white uniform with undivided attention. After all she was proud of being the most efficient nurse at Balrampur Hospital, and a good nurse had to be immaculately dressed.

Young Sabiha was too involved in her problem to be unnerved by Qudsia Begum's lack of attention. She continued to talk, and at last came out with the solution which her mother had found to the problem the family was facing right now.

"You know *Apa*," she pulled at Qudsia Begum's *anchal* to draw her attention, "*Ammi* and the rest of us have decided to get *Bhaijan* married again. If he has got one wife of his choice, he should get one wife of our choice also."

It was this remark that drew the scream from the hitherto inattentive woman. The charcoal iron nearly toppled off the *takhat*. And all that Qudsia Begum could do was to stare at this educated girl almost a generation younger than her. She said nothing more to Sabiha. Settling her *dupatta* on her greying hair, she said it was time for her namaz and moved towards the tap for her ablutions.

But that evening her namaz was said only mechanically. Qudsia Begum was in a daze. She felt that nothing had changed since she walked out of her husband's affluent home with nothing but the clothes she was wearing.

She remembered that evening all too vividly. The daylight was gradually paling into night when she heard a tonga stop at her gate and soon after she saw her husband Faiyaz enter the house with his new bride. There followed an atmosphere of quiet embarrassment about the house. For some time she got apologetic glances from her in-laws and sympathy from her servants and neighbours. But soon people became vocal. Her in-laws encouraged her by saying she had nothing to lose, she would be looked after well. Faiyaz was a nice boy, after all. He would put her on the same pedestal as his new bride.

But Qudsia Begum could not understand the logic of such a relationship. Between herself and Faiyaz there was place only for love, and love can only exist between one man and one woman. And then, one night Faiyaz quietly entered her room, just as he used to do. She was on the prayer mat saying her *isha* namaz. He settled down on her bed and waited for her to complete her prayers. She finished her prayers and walked to the *takhat* and sat down near the *paandan*.

"Qudsia, what worries you? Why don't you talk to me?" Qudsia Begum had imagined that he would never be able to meet her eye and that if she was ever directly accosted by him she would break down, but nothing of the sort happened. She could only feel ice forming round her heart.

"Qudsia, please listen to me, nothing has changed between us, I love you as much as I did before," Faiyaz mustered all the softness he could to console her. But she could bear no more.

"Liar," she shouted and turned her face with such disgust that Faiyaz felt quite insulted. His ego hurt by her indifference and coldness, he stood up, and declared. "How dare you behave like that with me? You are my wife."

And all that ice which had formed round her heart melted through her eyes. Qudsia Begum pulled her *nath* from her nose and threw it at Faiyaz's face and shouted, "*Kameene*, no man can be husband to more than one woman at the same time." She then rushed out of her room into the courtyard and into the kitchen, where she picked up the grinding stone and breaking her glass bangles she shouted, "This much for my *suhag* which had no meaning the moment you ceased to be faithful to me." Faiyaz and his mother froze where they were. And Qudsia Begum took a decision which few women in her place would have had the courage to take. She crossed the threshold of her husband's house never to look back again.

A knock at the door woke Qudsia Begum from her reverie. It was more than twenty years ago when she had lived through that nightmare, but her life that followed, though full of challenges, had brought her such satisfaction that she never regretted her decision. Her career as a nurse which had started amidst stiff opposition had brought her success, recognition and satisfaction. Could life with Faiyaz have given her that satisfaction, that confidence, and that self-respect? Qudsia Begum had her doubts.

The knock on the door became louder. It was Khilawan, the sweeper.

"Open *Bibi Ji*, Dularey is very ill." Dularey was Khilawan's seventh born and like the other six kids was always in frail health. Qudsia Begum knew she would have to go to Khilawan's house to see Dularey. She took out the medicine chest and poured out some milk in a bowl. Should the child require any nourishment Khilawan's hovel was not the place to find it.

She unlatched the door. "What is the matter, *Beta*? Don't get upset, have faith in Allah. Here, take this lock and put it on my door, I am rushing to your house."

Qudsia Begum knew her way around Kachcha Hata. She was considered a messiah in this *basti*. When she was returning home after treating little Dularey it was past midnight. She noticed that the lights were still on in Vakeel Sahib's house. Surprisingly a rickshaw was parked outside the house. There was some luggage on it.

"*Salaam, Apa.*" Chuttan the rickshaw puller flashed his yellow teeth in a friendly grin.

"Is someone going somewhere from Vakeel Sahib's house? Which train could be leaving at this unearthly hour?" Curious, she asked Chuttan.

Just then she saw Vakeel Sahib's son Arshad Mian approach the rickshaw with his newly married wife.

"I am leaving, *Apa*." Arshad Mian said.

"You are taking *dulhan* also?"

"Obviously. Wherever we go, we go together." And Qudsia Begum sensed that something serious had happened in the family. Arshad Mian continued. "*Ammi* and *Abba* didn't want me to have a family, they wanted me to have a harem," and he helped his wife into the seat and then sat down beside her. Both smiled at Qudsia Begum. There was no one at the door of that big house to say farewell to the couple. The lane where Vakeel Sahib's house stood was always dark and lonely. In the dead of night it looked lonelier and darker. But for Qudsia Begum suddenly the sun emerged in all its glory. As the rickshaw moved away, she turned towards her house and said, "Allah is great," and walked back with much greater confidence than she had ever done before.

The Whip

The Lucknow-wala hated to be away from Lucknow. He avoided leaving the city even for short periods and short distances. Exile till Kanpur, a distance of eighty miles, was an extreme and dreaded punishment given by the kings of Awadh to errant Lucknow citizens. But after the annexation of Awadh in 1856, when King Wajid Ali Shah was deposed and ordered to leave Lucknow, Calcutta became the city where Lucknow-walas loved to go, because it was there that their beloved King was exiled. He settled in Matiaburj and was allowed to live there as he wished. So, as expected, the King created a mini Lucknow, complete with Imambaras and mosques. He had a zoo there too, not as elaborate as the one he had in Lucknow, but his menagerie in Matiaburj too, attracted a lot of attention and was a source of interest for many. Houses came up for his courtiers and employees and hangers-on and life continued to move in as much royal a style as was possible with his annual rupees-twelve-lakh pension and permission to retain the title of King till his death. The British Crown had, reluctantly, allowed all this on advice of the Court of Directors.

Writers and poets, musicians and dancers followed their king to Calcutta. Even businessmen of Lucknow began looking towards Calcutta for a market. Migration to the eastern city was quite prominent. Noblemen who didn't want to settle there went there for part of the year, so that they could have *darshan* of their king without being disconnected from Lucknow.

Nawab Saeedudaulah, who was a descendant of the Kings of Awadh, was one such nobleman. He had a large establishment in Calcutta as he had in Lucknow. He shuttled between his two homes, as he wished and according to his convenience. This was at the end of the 19th century. The king lived in Calcutta for thirty-one years after the annexation and his exile, and died in 1887.

One beautiful evening Nawab Saeedudaulah was driving around on his stately two-horse carriage when the whip in the *coachwan's* hand broke into two. The streets of Calcutta were crowded and busy even at the end of the 19th century, unlike the cool and peaceful streets of Lucknow. The two horses pulling the carriage were not only well-bred and strong but had a tendency to become wild at the sight of crowds. Both the *coachwan* and his master thought it wise to stop at a store to buy a new whip. They drove around looking for such a shop. After some time they found one. It was late evening when the carriage stopped in front of the shop. The owner was locking up the place. He refused to open it .

"Yes I have a number of whips in the shop but it won't be worthwhile opening up the entire place just for a petty thing like a whip," he said to the *coachwan*, who informed his master and turned towards his seat to drive ahead. But his master asked him to call the owner of the shop. He wanted to have a word with him. The shop owner came and stood by the carriage after the usual salutations.

"What would be the price of all the goods in your shop?"

The shop keeper took some time to calculate and then said, "Sir the price of all the goods in the shop including the bag which is hanging on a peg on the wall is three lakh rupees."

"I will buy everything which is in the shop," the nawab said to the stunned shop owner. Then turning towards his *munshi*, who accompanied him and was sitting on the rear seat of the carriage, he said, "Munshiji give this gentleman rupees three lakhs immediately." The nawab gave the orders to his *munshi* in such a firm tone that the *munshi* couldn't dare to explain to his master the ridiculousness of the deal. He was left with no option but to pull out the amount from his bag and hand it over to the shop owner. By that time a bunch of beggars had collected around the nawab's carriage not just to see the tamasha but also hoping that they may get a paisa or two from the nawab.

Three lakh rupees in his hand, the shop owner handed to Nawab Sahib the key of the shop, a bag and a whip. What followed was something which no one expected. The nawab gave the key of the shop to his secretary who also accompanied him in the carriage.

"Open the shop," he said, "and distribute all there is in it among these beggars and come back to me empty handed." The orders given, the carriage of Nawab Saeedudaulah moved on with just the whip and the bag. The horses had hardly taken a few steps, when the shop owner came running after the carriage and pleaded before the nawab, "I just remembered sir, there are some very important papers in the bag which I need. I request you, most humbly, to give them back to me."

The shop owner's request was against the deal. Nawab Sahib could have easily refused, but he said, "Come tomorrow to my house and take them."

When Nawab Sahib and his staff reached home, the first thing his *munshi* did was to check up the contents of the bag. He found therein title deeds of a hotel, several houses and some lands. Munshiji informed his master about the papers in the bag and advised him thus: "*Huzoor,* you'll be well within the deal which you struck with the shop owner if you do not let him have anything from the bag. Your action will be within law and in all honesty. God has given you a golden opportunity to make the best of a bad deal."

"I have already told the shop owner that he can come and take whatever papers he wants from the bag. I cannot go back on my word," Nawab Sahib said and refused to hear anything more on the subject. The following morning when the shop owner came to Nawab Sahib's house, he was given his property papers without any further discussion.

At the end of all this, Nawab Saeedudaulah was as happy as ever, and absolutely satisfied and at peace with himself. He never cursed himself for having purchased a whip for three lakh rupees nor did he have any remorse for letting go that rare opportunity of turning a bad deal into a good bargain. On the contrary he was happy for ensuring that his horses did not get out of control and cause unpleasantness for the traffic on the road. He was happier still that he had kept his word.

Pensioner Royale

Nawab Sahib rushed impatiently to the door at the first knock. He could hardly wait for his gnarled and twisted fingers to unlatch the door. His face lit up to see Karamat the *rafoogar* who bent double to salute him. He handed him a big packet which contained Nawab Sahib's only *achkan*. Karamat was delivering it to the owner after darning it. Nawab Sahib's begum was herself excellent at stitching and tailoring. She had never taken professional help for repairing her husband's clothes. But on this occasion, the holes in the *achkan* were far too many and the time at her disposal limited. She had to complete the embroidery on a saree by the weekend and deliver it to Balmukund, the broker who brought clothes to her for being embroidered. Balmukund was a hard task and poor paymaster. He did not hesitate to fine her for any delay and of course never paid her her wages on time. Begum Sahib decided to concentrate only on the embroidery. She had to keep the kitchen fire burning.

Today Nawab Sahib was to go to the Waqf Board in Hussainabad to get his *wasiqa*, the pension given to the descendants of the kings of Awadh, which he collected annually.

If the help of the professional darner had not been taken, Nawab Sahib would have had to, God forbid, go out in a shabby *achkan*. So, now, when Nawab Sahib buttoned up his *achkan* and stood ready to leave, his confidence was high. He was sure that his appearance would not bring shame to the memory of his ancestors. Begum Sahib got up from her work and tied the *imam zamin* on his right arm for his safety and security. He was going out all alone after a long time. She thanked Allah for helping them keep up appearances. Nawab Sahib reminded her that Karamat had done a good job on his *achkan*. "May Allah bless him," Begum Sahib said graciously, and Nawab Sahib gently lifted the gunny bag curtain and was on his way. With one wave of his walking stick he hailed a rickshaw. Four rickshaw pullers rushed towards his door. Word had already got around that he was going to collect his pension. Nawab Sahib hated to disappoint poor people. He sat on one rickshaw and told the other three to follow him.

While the rickshaw rolled towards Hussainabad, Nawab Sahib was rolling out many a plan. This time he was determined to put his pension to good use. Begum Sahib needed a proper pair of spectacles and a warm shawl, and he deserved a new *achkan*. But before he got a new *achkan* for himself, there were gifts to be sent to his newly married granddaughter. Then both he and Begum Sahib needed proper blankets. Lucknow nights were getting too cold for the rags with which they covered themselves. These plans were in Nawab Sahib's mind when the rickshaw came to a halt in the dilapidated portico of the Waqf office. A dozen men with shabby clothes and polished manners rushed to welcome him. Nawab Sahib alighted from the rickshaw and amidst much fanfare reached the Cash Counter. He took his *wasiqa* of ₹138 which was paid to him at the rate of ₹11.50 per month. Pride was oozing out from every pore of his body. After all, this *wasiqa* and memories were the only two links with his royal and affluent past which were left with him. This paltry amount of money was the only certificate he had about his royal ancestry.

As Nawab Sahib turned from the cash counter, the same set of men, with shabby clothes and polished manners, surrounded him to say *khuda hafiz*. Nawab Sahib tipped them as lavishly as he could and boarded the rickshaw, this time to be mobbed by beggars. He could rescue himself only after he had been relieved of the major portion of his pension. At last he reached home. After paying the rickshaw on which he went and the other three which accompanied him, Nawab Sahib had only two ten-rupee notes left with him, which he quietly handed over to Begum Sahib. He had found her standing near the door, peeping out from a convenient hole in the gunny bag curtain. Begum Sahib was obviously waiting for him. She eagerly took the two notes and proudly put them in her *paandaan*.

The money had hardly reached the *paandaan* when a knock was heard on the door. This time Nawab Sahib appeared in no haste to open the door. But open the door he must, for he knew that it was Karamat *Rafoogar* who was at the door waiting to collect his darning charges. He asked his wife to hand him back the money. "We should pay the labourer his due even before the sweat on his brow dries up," he said. Begum Sahib agreed and handed him back the money as willingly as she had taken it.

When Nawab Sahib came back into the house after paying Karamat, his hands were empty. His pension was all spent, not a paisa remained, for the things he needed, and planned to buy. Like in the previous years, this year again, a new *achkan*, a shawl, spectacles and woollen blankets kept waiting for him in their respective shops. But Nawab Sahib was quite satisfied with how he spent his pension He had no regrets. He never lost hope. He was sure his next annual *wasiqa* would fetch him all that he and Begum Sahib needed to keep themselves alive and their *izzat* intact. He said to himself, "At least no one will say this man does not behave like royalty. No one will say that no generosity is left in the children of the kings of Awadh." With these thoughts in mind, Nawab Sahib lay down on his bed, relaxed and satisfied with the day's happenings, though he was already looking forward to the lucky day next year when he would get his annual *wasiqa*.

Begum Sahib was also not dissatisfied with the heads on which the *wasiqa* was spent. She was nursing a hope though, that Balmukund, like Nawab Sahib, would start paying his workers the wages for their labour before the sweat dried on their brows!

Khansamas[*]

The young man, who runs the immensely popular non-vegetarian eatery outside the Press Club, was talking to me about his restaurant. Not once did he refer to his cooks as cooks or khansamas or *bawarchis* or even as *rasoiyas*. He consistently called them, *karigar*! I was taken aback. The man talking to me was in the food industry and the city was Lucknow! For God's sake, you can't just use any word you like for any profession and get away with it. There was, no doubt, a time in Lucknow when *bawarchis* and khansamas had raised cooking to an art form. Dishes were all but crafted. But no cook ever claimed to be a craftsman or aspired to be called one. The *bawarchikhanas* of the nawabs and of the aristocracy were not just kitchens to cook food but laboratories where research in the culinary art was always in progress. Khansamas invented new dishes and received rich rewards and titles. Mamdu Bawarchi invented the Sheermal sometime in the mid 19th century, the likes of which no other *bawarchi* in any other city could produce.

The cooks of the nawabs and the nobility were given staggering salaries, and total freedom to pursue their work

*   This article first appeared in the *Times of India* (Lucknow edition) in July 2010.

along with an army of helpers. It was the *bawarchis* who laid down the terms and conditions of employment which, even the crowned heads accepted. There was also an unwritten law that the employer would sanction whatever quantities of ingredients the cook demanded, without asking any questions or expressing any doubts. No wonder the cooks could produce dishes which were a delight for the tastebuds, and yet, easy to digest. The Lucknow aristocracy took great pleasure in extending invitations to elaborate meals where some dishes were camouflaged. If the guest could not make out what the item was, the host would feel highly elated. *This* guessing game was played as late as 1998, at a dinner hosted by the commissioner, Central Excise for the delegates attending a meeting of the United Nations Sub-commission at Lucknow concerning narcotic drugs and psychotropic substances. The union minister of state for Finance was one of the guests. The dessert was a *"kheer"* and the guests had to guess what the *kheer* was made of. None of them could tell that the *kheer* was made of garlic!

In the homes of the *shurfa* (plural for *shareef*, middle class, could be upper middle class and well educated) a good *bawarchi* could be hired for ₹15 per month, till the early 1950s. But there had to be a helper in the kitchen for grinding masala, cutting vegetables, washing dishes and keeping the kitchen clean. The *bawarchi* was given food, enough for at least two, and new clothes on festivals. His illnesses were attended to. *If* he needed a place to stay, he could stay in some part of the house. But before he got an appointment he had to pass a difficult test.

My parents' menu for a test was a korma, *dhuli* (washed) *mash ki daal, khushka* and chapattis. I remember a cook was rejected because he put turmeric in the korma. Even a novice knew that turmeric is put in the masala when vegetables are added to the meat, never in korma which is only mutton pieces in gravy. By the late sixties khansamas became a rare species. You were lucky if you could get one for ₹100 a month. Expecting them to consent for a test was unthinkable. In the years that followed, khansamas stopped training their children for the profession.

Going back to "*karigari*," the cake baked for my fifth birthday was by all standards an example of high level "*karigari*". The *karigar* was a khansama whose name no one in the family knew. We called him "Ismail ke Abba". His estranged wife Rahiman referred to him as that. Rahiman lived in our house. I am not very clear what work she did for us. I remember her as someone who told interesting stories and sang songs which she insisted were *thumris* and *dadras*. She told us how "Ismail ke Abba" (her husband) left her for an ugly ayah who worked for the same *angrez* as her husband.

It was Ismail, her son, who convinced his father to bake that special cake for the occasion. The cake had five tiers. As I placed the knife on the topmost tier, my mother holding my hand all the while, a slice, which looked like a door, fell aside, and out flew to safety, a live sparrow from the cake!! There was a thunderous applause from the guests. People forgot the birthday girl and Ismail ke Abba, who stood proudly at the door, became the hero of the day. A little later, when my father requested him to move in, as our khansama, Ismail ke Abba was not amused. He had worked only for the *angrez* sahibs and left cooking when they left. "*Adjustments with Hindustanis*" may not be possible, he felt! He spoke no more, collected his tips, bent double to make his salaams and left!

Kallan ki Lat

The photograph on the cover is of a British cemetery in Lucknow called Kallan ki Lat. It is not the whole cemetery, just a part of it, which our very ordinary camera captured in the year 1984, from the balcony of our house which is right opposite the cemetery, and very close to Aminabad.

Even from that strategic angle the camera could not cover the enormous place, spread over acres of land and surrounded by a fortress like wall. In Lucknow there are many British cemeteries but this is the largest. I have seen British cemeteries in Aurangabad, in Bangalore and in many other cities including the Park Street cemetery of Kolkata. But none are so huge as this one was, nor do they have such magnificent funerary structures which this cemetery had. Most of the graves in Kallan ki Lat had stately obelisks built over them. The tallest obelisk in the picture is the one built over the remains of Colonel John Collins, affectionately called Kallan Sahib by Lucknow-walas.

Collins was the Resident in the court of Nawab Vazeer Sadat Ali Khan from 1806 to 1807. He was an old India hand. He joined the East India Company's Bengal Rifles in 1770. Though he had a short stint as Resident of Awadh he was Resident at the court of Daulat Rao Sindhia also. There he found the ruler plotting against the Company, despite the Treaty of Bassein. As a result war was declared against Daulat Rao. Collins was associated with Awadh, even before he became its Resident, in some capacity or the other, since the time of Nawab Vazeer Shuja-ud-Daulah. Qurratul Ain Hyder, the famous Urdu novelist, has written about him in one of her novels and even given a sketch of his Lat. He came very young to India and never married.

He died suddenly, while still in office, on the 18th of June 1807. Till that time the Resident in Awadh had not become as important as he did subsequently, particularly after the nawab vazeers were given the titles of King by the East India company. When Collins was the Resident of Awadh protocol did not allow his chair to be placed at the same level as the *masnad* of the nawab vazeer. And yet Sadat Ali Khan made the rare gesture of being present at Collin's funeral. He did not only give an enormous plot of land for his burial but also built a gigantic memorial over his grave, after taking permission from the East India Company.

This tomb is not like the ones built over Muslim graves. It is an obelisk, a tall tapering column 60ft high from the ground, made of *lakhauri* bricks and lime with stucco decorations. This towering column was the highest building in Lucknow at that time and continued to be so for a long time. In 1837 King Mohammad Ali Shah began the construction of another tower like structure which was to be used for sighting the moon. According to the plan, it was to have seven storeys and was called *sathkhanda*. People of Lucknow believed that the

Sathkhanda would rise over Kallan Sahib's obelisk but it was not to be. King Mohammed Ali Shah died in 1842 when just three storeys were ready. His son and successor, King Amjad Ali Shah did not care to complete it.

In Kallan ki Lat cemetery, near Kallan Sahib's obelisk, there was a round *baradari* type of structure though it had only six *dars* (openings) and two beautiful *chattries* on the roof. This round airy building was presumably used to rest the coffins while the burial arrangements were made. Perhaps the funeral prayers were also said there, because there was no church in the vicinity. The nearest church was in the Residency. All the graves did not have obelisks over them. Some of them were flat but were not like the present Christian graves. They looked like chunks cut out from a loaf of bread. There was also a tomb with four *dars* near the round structure, which did not appear to have a body buried under the ground but had a box like structure placed over the ground and pegged to it with lime.

Lat is a Hindi/Urdu word for a tower-like structure. Very high officials were also referred to as Lat Sahib. The governor, for instance, is till now called Lat Sahib by the common man. Collins being the Resident of Awadh was Lat Sahib, because he was the highest representative of the Company. In some records this cemetery is mentioned as Lat Kallan ki Lat, meaning the Lat of Lat Sahib Kallan. But the people have always called the cemetery and the mohalla which developed around it, Kallan ki Lat and at times just Lat Kallan.

This cemetery was a kind of Westminster Abbey where people of some consequence were buried. Yet there are no records to show as to who they were. Names and epitaphs which were inscribed must have faded away over time. Only Kallan Sahib's Lat had the following inscription till quite recently.

In memory

of

Colonel John Collins,

Resident in the Court of Lucknow 1806-7

Died 18th June 1807.

It is also a well known fact that Colonel R. Wilcox the astronomer royal who served four kings, and who built the observatory during the reign of King Naseer-ud-din Haider which was called Taron wali Kothi, died in 1848 and was buried in Kallan ki Lat. Rosie Llewellyn-Jones has mentioned in a chapter of her book *Engaging Scoundrels* that Frederick, the infant son of another Resident, Mordaunt Ricket was also buried in the Kallan ki Lat cemetery in 1828. This must have been during the reign of King Naseer-ud-din Haider. Though a large amount of space still remained unused the Kallan ki Lat cemetery was closed by the year 1858.

Colonel John Collins' grave occupied the most prominent place in the cemetery. From the beautiful iron gate, one could get a full view of it. Though Sadat Ali Khan the Nawab Vazeer, who donated the land, intended the cemetery to be for all denominations of Christians but most of the graves are said to be those of Catholics. It was also looked after by the Catholic Diocese of Lucknow till 1992 when the cemetery was desecrated.

The upkeep of the cemetery was very good till the 1950s after which, it deteriorated. Though there was hardly any maintenance in the later years the cemetery retained its grandeur till the 1980s. Azim ullah a resident of the mohalla around the cemetery was hired as a chowkidar, perhaps by the bishop of Lucknow, from the 1930s. He held the post till the mid-1980s when a younger chowkidar was appointed in his place. Azim ullah lived in a house, of his own, outside the cemetery. But surprisingly in the 1980s he moved inside the Kallan ki Lat, with his family and allowed space to a relative of his for a month, every year, to manufacture *siwai* before Eid. After this, people started viewing the cemetery as a place where the homeless could move in. The new chowkidar also moved into the cemetery after building a house for himself. It is believed that it was he who convinced the authorities to plot the vacant land and sell it to Christians. The vacant land was plotted. Some Christians did buy the plots, but never moved in. In course of time, they resold the land to others who moved in after building shanties on the vacant land.

Then suddenly, in 1992, a horde of antisocial elements descended upon the cemetery, attacked and demolished the graves and built houses for themselves anywhere they pleased. The whole cemetery was razed to the ground, but surprisingly, the demolition squads could do no harm to the 185-year-old Kallan Sahib's Lat. It still stands there unseen and unnoticed surrounded by ugly one brick tenements, some of them several storeys high. Only its pinnacle sadly peeps out from behind those houses. In recent years the fortress like wall which surrounded the cemetery has been broken at many places to create convenient entrances and exits, for the almost fifty families who live there.

Two hundred and five years ago when Kallan Sahib left this world and was given a permanent residence under that majestic Lat, he slept there in splendid isolation, not because there were no other graves there yet, but there was no habitation either. People moved into that area just around the time of the mutiny. Though Jhao Lal, a minister of Asif-ud-Daulah, had sometime earlier built a road to connect the Residency to that area perhaps because he had constructed a haveli which stretched from that road to a place very near Kallan Sahib's resting place. I think that was the distant end of the city which was found suitable only for graveyards. The road which led to Kallan Ki Lat turned right after reaching its high iron gate and then in another minute turned left and passed before a banyan tree. Under the banyan tree there are two pairs of graves. Two of them are believed to be those of Syed Salar Ghazi and his nephew. The graves were referred to as Mamu Bhanje ki Qabar and the area around it is also called Mamu Bhanje ki Qabar. There was a Muslim graveyard behind the Kallan ki Lat, (also desecrated decades before the Kallan ki Lat cemetery) adjacent to its rear wall, and at a two minutes walk from there, was a majestic tomb where lay buried a Muslim woman called Gori Bi.

The place was sparsely populated till the 1930s, the 1940s and even 1950s. People would avoid going out after dark in that area, for they believed that Kallan Sahib would be loitering around in the night, begging for '*makhan roti*'. Educated people felt those rumours were floated by thieves and money snatchers so that they could do their work and put the blame on Kallan Sahib's ghost.

My parents had an interesting incident to narrate about Kallan Sahib's ghost. My father used to wear solar hats. He once threw his hat into Kallan ki Lat because it had got soaked in rain and bought another for himself. Some months later my mother had cooked *shahi tukras* as dessert for dinner. She wanted to share the delicacy with my father's sister, who lived in Kachcha Hata, a locality on the other side of Kallan Ki Lat and just five minutes' walk from our house. This was in the mid-1940s. She told Channoo, the kitchen helper, to take the dish to her house. He begged my mother to send someone else, or wait for daybreak.

"Why?" my mother asked.

"It is quite dark, Begum Sahib. This is just the time when Kallan Sahib starts roaming around asking for *makhan roti*. The *gali* to *Bahen* Sahib's house is very dangerous."

"Then go by the Mamu Bhanje ki Qabar road. It will take you just two minutes more," my mother suggested.

"But ultimately *I'll have* to reach *Bahen* Sahib's house. I'm told he is seen there very often. He has to cross her house to go to Gori Bi's tomb." Channoo was almost shivering. But it appeared he knew Kallan Sahib's entire nocturnal ramblings.

"But why does he have to go to her tomb?"

"She is his wife *Huzoor*." My mother laughed, but my father, who was listening to the entire conversation, came out into the veranda and took the dish from my mother's hand and said, "I'll take it but ... Channoo!"

"Ji *Huzoor*."

"You'll come with me."

And Channoo went shivering with my father through the lane which ran adjacent to the wall of Kallan ki Lat. On the other side were the ruins of a big house which occupied the entire length of the street.

When both men had walked half the length of the street they heard a voice repeatedly saying, *"Ham makhan roti mangta,"* coming from inside the ruins. Channoo started running and then my father felt someone walking behind him. Father turned around, torch in hand, and saw a tall man with a walking stick and solar hat on his head. He did feel shaken for a minute but then he shouted, *"Kaun ho tum"*, and the person ran in the opposite direction. As he turned around to run, he dropped his hat, which my father picked up and realised that it was the same hat which he had thrown into Kallan ki Lat some months ago, when it had got soaked in rain. Father even caught the man and discovered that he was the son of a schoolteacher who lived in the neighbourhood. He said he was only playing a joke! Channoo was traced, minus the dish of *shahi tukras*, two hours later, at the Aminabad Post Office. He had gone on running and stopped only when he fainted. He developed high fever and remained in bed for a week. Channoo never believed that it was not Kallan Sahib's ghost who was asking for *makhan roti* but a young man from the neighbourhood.

Today no one speaks of Kallan Sahib's nocturnal activities. He is a wise soul, or has become wise over the years. With crowds pressing round him he knows he cannot afford to leave his Lat to loiter around. He may get stuck in a traffic jam and come back to find his Lat gone!

Lucknow: Lost and Found in its Bylanes[*]

Forty years in civil service convinces you that you cannot be a permanent resident of any city. Just when you get used to any place you have to move on and set up house in yet another place, whether you like it or not. You may also never get a chance to work in your own home town.

But I was lucky. I got several stints, long and short, in Lucknow. That was when, I saw the city expand, become dirty, more crowded and the fabled Lakhnavi *"zubaan"* acquire a touch which was not welcome to the ears. I saw loyal Lucknowites leaving Lucknow for metros in search of better prospects for themselves or for their children. I also saw rural folk pouring into Lucknow for jobs, which were not there.

And yet when retirement deprived me of *ghoda*, *gaadi* and *kursi*, it was Lucknow, I heard, beckoning me. Strangely enough, I did not even ponder over the call, like people do over all invitations. I just rushed towards the *sarzameen*, as Sadat Khan had done long long ago, in the early twenties of the 18th century. But Sadat Khan, that Persian adventurer, from Nishapur, had reason, and a good enough one, to leap towards Lucknow. He

* This piece appeared in the *Times of India*, Lucknow edition on Tuesday, 18 May 2010.

had, in his hand, an order appointing him as the subedar of Awadh and he also had destiny on his side, willing to make him founder of a dynasty that was to rule over Awadh for 134 years.

What reason, did I have to leave Delhi where I had at least half a dozen childhood friends, a dozen other good friends, waiting to ensure that I was never lonely? Delhi could have been for me, a replay of school, and a replay of youth. It could have been a game of Power. In Delhi prospects never fail and hope lives forever.

Still, I chose Lucknow over Delhi and reached Gomtinagar, where, I had built a house more than a decade ago. But alas, it did not take very long for me to start regretting my decision. Not that I was missing Delhi. It was Lucknow I was missing. I did not find Lucknow in Gomtinagar. The few moments of delight which I experienced were when I entered the area. The magnificent well-lit exotic buildings, the six-lane bridge and the dazzling lights, bordering miles and miles of roads, took my breath away. The "Queen's Necklace" on Marine Drive in Mumbai struck me as a poor cousin of this endless string of lights, which stretched before me. But even in the midst of this spectacular show, there was nothing of Lucknow that I could find. Even the Gomti was not visible.

I had no option but to go in search of Lucknow. I ventured towards Hazratganj, crossing roads, heavy with construction of high-rise buildings. I could not make out which well-known *Kothis* were felled to make those not very pleasing flats. And then the 'Ganj'. One or two new buildings stood alongside dilapidated structures covered with neon signs. The road between them was strewn with parked cars while slow traffic manoeuvred between them, somehow. There was no "Mayfair," no "Kwality"; even the heritage building of the Hazratganj Police Station was not there. This was, definitely, not the 'Ganj' which was the pride of Lucknow.

And the less said about Aminabad the better. The place was suffocating. Shopping was like a punishment. The shopkeepers had banished the Lucknow style of salesmanship, which their refugee grandfathers had wasted no time in acquiring, leaving the tragedies of Partition behind them.

I was eager to see Aminuddaulah Park, also called "Jhande Wala Park", where many a landmark speech had been delivered during the freedom struggle. It was there, that Nehru, in 1950, had said "Aaraam Haraam Hai," while addressing a crowd, making it the slogan of the 50s. I couldn't make out what the park was used for now. May be for parking of cars.

My keenness to find Lucknow took me to the Imambaras, the Maqbaras, Sikandarbagh, Qaiserbagh and La Martiniere. These buildings which withstood the hostility of the British during the First War of Independence, with poise and patience, appeared on the verge of collapse. The *restoration* of the Asifi Imambara was no cause for satisfaction either. Even the latest Master Plan has no consideration for heritage.

My eagerness to find Lucknow had by now turned into despair. For no reason, I turned towards Moulviganj, where a kind, but hungry dog started following me. I felt obliged and decided to buy him some milk. I found a shop in a bylane leading to Rassi Batan. The milk was given in a *kullhar*, which I placed before the dog and got up to move on, when I heard someone call, "Baby," and again "Baby."

I didn't see a child in the vicinity, so I turned around. To my utter surprise, I found an old man calling out to me. Strange! Doesn't he see silver in my hair, I wondered. I looked at him enquiringly. There was something familiar about his eyes and about his smile.

"Baby don't you remember me; I am 'ice-cream wala'. I used to stand outside Bhaktin School, at home time. (Loreto Convent was called Bhaktin School by the uneducated people, a reference to the devout nuns running the school.) You always bought ice-cream from my *thela*. You liked chock bar best, na baby?"

"Yes, I did, even now I like it best." I recognised him immediately; my joy knew no bounds, "At that time a chock bar was for four *annas*. Now it is very expensive and not as good," I volunteered unabashed.

"I will get you a chock bar as it used to be, and you won't have to pay even four *annas*. You tell me where you live. Earlier, you lived opposite Kallan ki Lat."

"Yes, I did, but how did you know?"

"I knew where all the children who bought my ice-cream lived," he said.

I was stunned; I was delighted; I was ecstatic; I was reassured; I had found Lucknow.

Glossary

Aaraam Haraam Hai: Jawaharlal Nehru's famous catchphrase meaning 'Rest is wicked/blasphemous.

Abba: Father.

Achkan: Something like a Shervani a long coat worn by men over Kurta and Churidar Paijama.

Ada: Grace, style, panache.

Adab Arz: A polite way of greeting. Literally meaning Salutations to you. *Adab* is a salutation and *Arz* is a humble way of saying that I am speaking.

Adab baja laata hun: It simply means I pay my respects. It is a very polite way of wishing an older or much respected person. This is a typically Lucknow way of uttering the salutation.

Adab: This is a salutation developed in Lucknow to be used by all regardless of the community they belonged to, because *asalamalaikum* was used by Muslims for Muslims and *Jai Ram Ji ki*, and *Ram Ram* was uttered by Hindus for Hindus.

Adda: Wooden frame holding the cloth—velvet, satin, etc—tight for Zardozi embroidery.

Agni: The sacred fire.

Alhamdulillah: Allah be praised.

Ammi: Affectionate form of address of Amma or mother.

Anchal: Two ends of the dupatta, or the end of the saree covering the head. This part of the garment is more decorative.

Angrez: British / Englishman.

Anna: One-sixteenth of a rupee in old Indian currency. Obsolete now.

Apa: Sister.

Assalamalaikum: Salutations. It means, "peace be on you". It is a salutation by one Muslim to another.

Aziz: Near and dear one.

Baby ikanni lo kitab do: Take an anna and give us your book.

Badi: Elder.

Bagghi: One horse carriage.

Baithak: Sitting room or the room where the visitors, especially male visitors, are entertained.

Baja farmaya Huzoor nay: Huzoor is right.

Baji: Muslims of Northern India call their older sisters Baji.

Baradari: A building with twelve openings, doors or entrances.

Bare Shehzade: Elder prince.

Basti: Locality.

Bawarchi: Cook, the word has an Urdu/Persian origin explained in detail above in the story 'When a Jagir Went Abegging'.

Bawarchi: Cook. *Khan-e-saman* was a very high official who was in charge of the entire household effects in the home of a noble/aristocrat. Gradually the people started referring to their cook as khansama. Perhaps it was the British who started the wrong use of the word.

Bawarchikhana: Kitchen.

Bela: A variety of jasmine flower.

Bepurdagi: Without *purdah*.

Beta: Son.

Bhagtin: Wife of a *bhagat*, a devotee one who practises religious rites and ceremonies.

Bhaijan: Affectionate form of address or reference to one's brother. 'Jan' is a suffix added on to denote affection and/or respect.

Bhaiya: Brother, respectful form of address of an outsider.

Bibi Ji: Respectful address for seniors, the elderly or the women of the house. Equivalent to Madame.

Biradari: Community; clan.

Bitiya: Daughter.

Burqa: Is the over-garment worn from head to toe over the normal garments by women to cover themselves.

But ke rahega Hindustan: Partition slogan by communalists fanning pro-Pakistan sentiments meaning 'Hindustan (India) will be divided' or more correctly 'We will agree to nothing short of division of the nation into Hindu and Muslim segments'.

Chachajan: Uncle, father's brother.

Chachi: Aunt, the wife of father's brother.

Chaliswan: The fortieth day ceremony following death.

Chattries: Umbrella like structures of stone and lime erected on top of any roof.

Chote Shehzade: Younger prince.

Coachwan: Driver of the coach or horse-driven carriage.

Dadras: Genre of classical Hindustani music songs.

Dar: Opening or door.

Darshan: Literally seeing or sighting. Refers to paying a courtesy call on a dignitary or spotting a dignitary or God.

Dastarkhwan: Dinner spread.

Deorhi: The place at the point of entrance of the house. It is normally a covered area. This word can also be used as the synonym for a haveli or a palace.

Dhuli: Literally washed; with reference to pulses it refers to the lentil after the skin has been removed and the pulse split into two.

Doli: A small palanquin.

Dulai: like a blanket or *razai*/quilt with a very thin layer of cotton spread between two stretches of cloth. In Lucknow it is used to cover oneself at night when it is not very cold.

Dulhan: Bride.

Dupatta: The two-metre or even longer cloth thrown over a salwar-churidar-gharara-kameez covering the head and upper part of the body.

Farkhati: Term for divorce, used by the uneducated classes.

Farmaiye: A polite way of asking the other person to speak. For instance: Please proceed; Tell me please.

Fateha: A verse in the Holy Quran which is recited for the departed soul to rest in peace.

Firangi: Literally a foreigner; in the pre-Independence context a foreign soldier or officer.

Gaadi: Carriage, Car, Mode of transport.

Gali: Lane.

Gharib Nawaz: Saviour for the destitute and the poor.

Gharibparvar: Messiah of the poor.

Ghazals: Poems.

Ghoda: Horse.

Ghunghat: The end of the saree covering the head and face like a veil.

Ghungroos: Strings of small bells tied by dancers on their feet.

Golgappa: Indian savoury snack, small poori-like in shape, filled with boiled potato cubes, boiled chickpeas and spice-flavoured water, considered a spicy delicacy.

Gulam: Slave, humble servant.

Ham makhan roti mangta: I am asking for bread and butter. Give me bread and butter.

Hans ke liya hai Pakistan, ladke lenge Hindustan: Partition slogan, by pro-Pakistan communalists meaning 'Pakistan was obtained with a smile, but Hindustan will also be taken back by us with a fight/we will not give up without a fight to get back Hindustan. Some people also see a pun on the word '*Ladke*' which also means boys or young men (our sons) who will subsequently take Hindustan too.

Haramiyon: Bastards.

Haveli: Mansion

Hazir hai: polite way of saying that it is here/it is available.

Hindustanis: People of Hindustan or India.

Hukka Pani: Literally means hookah and water but in this context, together the words connote excommunication and ostracising from the community.

Huzoor: A respectful form of address; Sir.

Ikka: Single-seater horse carriage.

Imam Zamin: Some money is tied to a band of cloth and tied on the right arm of a person who is going on a long journey or on an important mission. When the journey/mission is completed the money is removed from the band and given to the poor or needy. The person is actually given into the care of Imam Raza this way.

Insha Allah: Allah willing; God-willing.

Izzat: Honour.

Jagir: Landholding, title to land.

Janamaz: Prayer mat.

Jaroor Huzoor jaroor, bhagwan kasam jaroor: Definitely Sir, definitely, upon God's word most definitely.

Jeeti rahiye khush rahiye: (May you) Live long, be happy

Jhande Wala Park: There is a park in Lucknow of this name where during the Freedom struggle and later political leaders and freedom fighters used to address big crowds. It was called Aminuddaulah Park earlier. Now it is a car park.

Jharh-phoonk: A ritual aimed at driving away evil spirits or malefic influences possessing a person causing mental illness or serious diseases like jaundice.

Jhuggi: Hovel; hut; shanty.

Kacheri: A district court or high court.

Kahan gaye the: Where had you gone to?

Kameene: A swear word meaning 'lowly one'.

Kankaiya and dor: Kite and string.

Karigar: Craftsman.

Karigari: Craftsmanship.

Kaun ho tum: Who are you?

Khala Amma: Aunt, mother's sister.

Kharch: Spending money, stipend.

Kheer: Sweet dish with porridge-like consistency usually made of rice or pulses but can be made of anything that the cook's imagination can whip up and camouflage.

Khuda Hafiz: Goodbye, equivalent of "God with you" or "God protect you".

Khushka: Boiled rice.

Kotha: A courtesan's house or place of entertainment.

Kothis: Huge single-storeyed houses.

Kulhar: Clay or earthenware cup or flat dish.

Kulia: A narrow covered gully within a house connecting it with another. It could also be a very narrow gully outside.

Kursi: Literally chair but generally refers to seat of power in government lingo.

Kurtis: Waist-long kurtas.

Lakhauri: Very small oblong bricks sold one lakh for a rupee in the 19th century.

Lehngas: Ankle length Indian long skirts.

Lucknavi: Belonging to Lucknow/of Lucknow

Maghrib Namaz: Evening prayers.

Majlis: Any gathering, get-together, in this case to pray for the departed soul.

Makhan Roti: Butter and bread.

Mamu Bhanje ki Qabar: Tombstone of the uncle and nephew. (Mama is the maternal uncle and Bhanja is sister's son).

Mamujan: Uncle, mother's brother.

Mardana: Masculine.

Mash ki daal: A particular variety of lentils.

Masnad: Literal meaning is round pillow. In this case the place where the Nawab vazeer sat.

Maund: A measure of weight approximately forty seers.

Meher: Settlement agreed upon, at the time of the wedding, to be given to the bride. It should be paid immediately after the consummation of the marriage.

Mehfil: A party, a get together, a gathering for a function.

Mere Bachchon: Literally 'My Children'. In this context means an endearment like 'My dears/My darlings.'

Mohalla: Neighbourhood; locality.

Mohtarma: Madame, Lady.

Mokha: an informal opening in the wall.

Mubarak: Fortunate.

Mujra: The word *mujra* actually means to pay respects. The respect is paid to the people present in the audience in the form of dance, which is done in the Kathak dance form.

Munshi: An official who does secretarial work.

Musalmans: Reference to Muslims in the vernacular.

Namaz of shukrana: Prayer for thanksgiving

Nana Abba: Grandfather. Mother's father.

Nashist gah: Performance area in a courtesan's quarters.

Nath uthrai: This is a ceremony which initiates the girl into the profession of *tawaifs*. The *nath* (nose-ring, jewellery worn on the nose) is removed by the male who pays the agreed amount to the girl or to the madame of the *kotha* and the girl remains with him for the agreed period. Thereafter the girl is free to perform and work as she likes. This ceremony is typical to the upper class *tawaifs* who are called *deredar tawaifs*.

Nath: Nose-ring.

Nawabi: Pertaining to nawabs.

Nawan: Feminine gender of Nai, the barber; the barber's wife

Nikah: A Muslim marriage. It is the ceremony where a man and woman are joined in holy wedlock by a qazi who is an official to perform marriages.

Paandaan: A box with compartments for storing betel leaves, betel nuts, lime, cardamom, cloves and other condiments used in paan, the prepared betel leaves.

Paigham: A proposal of marriage. The proposal goes from the boy's side to the girl's parents.

Paikarma: Circumambulation; rolling on one's body from home to the temple and circumambulating a temple's premises.

Paisa: One-hundredth of a rupee now, earlier, before the metric system there were four paisas in an anna and sixteen anna in a rupee.

Panchas: The village elders participating in the panchayat and passing decisions.

Parathas: Shallow fried rotis

Pashmina: Wool from pashmina sheep, considered very soft and warm.

Pehalvan: Indian wrestler.

Peshkar: A court official usually in the clerical or lower cadres.

Phuphi: Aunt, father's sister.

Purdah-nashin: one who remains in *purdah* or observes *purdah*.

Purdah: A screen or curtain. Muslim women of genteel breeding observe *purdah* i.e. they appear behind a screen (or burqa) while interacting with all men who are not from the immediate family. The system of Purdah was adopted to protect women and their dignity. In Arabia after the advent of Islam women could go about their work with a chadar or Aba which did not cover their faces totally. Only hair and half the face were covered. Burqa which covered the whole face and body, originated from Turkey. It is believed Purdah came to India with Muslims. The practice was actually prevalent in Rajasthan much before their arrival.

Qabristan: Muslim graveyard.

Raanga: A cheap metal alloy resembling gold in colour
Rafoogar: Darner/One who darns clothes.
Rasoiya: Cook, origin Hindi.
Rehne deejye: Let it be; forget it.
Rickshawala: Cycle rickshaw puller.
Riyaz: Practice referring to dance and music lessons.
Roghni Rotis: Rotis or Indian bread where the dough is kneaded with milk and ghee instead of plain water.
Rukhsati: The formal ceremony or function for departure of the bride to the bridegroom's house.

Sadhvi: A female ascetic; feminine gender of sadhu
Sarauta: Betel-nut cutter.
Sarzameen: The land where our ancestors lived and died.
Sathkhanda: A structure with seven sections, storeys or divisions.
Seer: A measure of weight in olden times, little less than a kilo.
Shahi Tukras: A sweet made with fried bread pieces floated in thick condensed and sweetened milk.
Shalukas: Full-sleeved quilted waistcoats.
Shareef: Well-educated, genteel folk of good breeding and birth/lineage.
Shehzade Huzoor: Prince.
Shehzadi Begum: Princess.
Shijra: Family tree.
Shurfa: Plural of sharif meaning the urbane, genteel folk.

Siwai: Vermicelli.

Suhag: Married status, symbols of a married woman.

Supari: Betel nut or areca nut.

Takhat: Wooden bench or bed.

Talaq: Divorce.

Taluqedar: They held large land holdings, collected land revenue and gave the state their share. The taluqedars also looked after the law and order of the area.

Taron wali Kothi: Literally the house of stars, planetarium.

Tawaif: Courtesan.

Tehmad: Lungi, waistcloth.

Tehzeeb: Innate decency and genteel breeding; finesse; elan.

Thela: Handcart with handles pushed by peddlers hawking their ware.

Thumris: Genre of classical Hindustani music songs.

Tongawala: Driver of a tonga, a carriage seating four passengers apart from the driver.

Tunday: A person with one amputated arm is called a Tunda/Tunday in Hindi/Urdu.

Ustad: Maestro.

Vakalat: Practice of Law. *Vakeel* is a lawyer, *vakalat* is his profession.

Vilayat: Literally means a foreign country. But in British India generally referred to England.

Walima: The reception given, with a meal, by the bridegroom after the marriage has been consummated.

Wasiqa: The pension given to the descendants, servants and retainers of nawabs, promised for eternity. A loan was given by the Begums of Awadh (mother and grandmother of Asif-ud-Daulah) to the East India Company and later on also by King Ghaziuddin Haider. The wasiqa is given from this amount.

Yaar: Literally friend. Used colloquially in Urdu/Hindi conversations as an equivalent of the casual 'man'.

Zanankhana: Female quarters of a Muslim household where men, except those of immediate family are barred entry.

Zardozi karigar: Craftsman specialising in Zardozi embroidery.

Zardozi: Zar means precious metals (gold and silver), dozi means stitching. It is embroidery on velvet, silk, satin and chiffon with gold and silver threads.

Ziledar: He is an official under the Zamindar who has an area of land which he looks after on behalf of the zamindar/taluqedar.

Zubaan: Literally tongue or lingo. In the Lucknow context it refers to the cultured and refined language used by the gentry and commoners alike.